A Ghetto Love Story 3
Written by Author Tina Marie

Acknowledgements

I would first like to thank God for giving me this gift of writing and for providing me with every blessing I have received this far and will receive in the future.

I want to thank my family, my fiancé Jay for putting up with all the late nights and my crazy moods while I am writing. To my kids Jashanti, Jaymarni and Jasheer I want you to know that I work so hard so you can have it all. I want to thank all of my Pen Sisters no matter what company you are in for all of the love, support and for always helping to push me to my next goal, I appreciate you all.

To the crew, my sisters, Sharome, Shante, and Andrea I just want to say I love you all. Ladora you are the world's best little sister I love you and I believe in you keep pushing that number 1 is coming your way. Demetrea you are always there when I need to vent, cry or celebrate and I would do anything for you, love you lots!

To my Bad & Boujie team you came into my life at a time when I felt like I was alone in this writing ish. I guess God knew who I needed and when. I love you ladies to the moon and back. Thanks for all the calls, texts, laughter and tears and for showing me the definition of real friends. (I know all ya'll thug asses crying).

A special thank you to Tyanna for being a constant sweetheart and motivator. Chanique J for always having my back and my front, and Author Natavia, for being my friend, and one of my favorite authors all in one. Rikenya you have such a pure and kind heart, you are the kind of friend to be cherished and I do cherish you.

Nisey, I just have to say, Sis, you're the best. You know my schedule better than me and make me stick to it and never allow me to make excuses. Quanisha, you're a bomb assistant/admin. You don't let me forget a thing and handle all the grunt work so I can write. Love you, boo. Keke you have become my life line and even when your bossy I still love you. Sweets there would be no book without you, even when you told me to rewrite a whole chapter I still loved you! Keri this book is for you boo!!! I hope you love how your character turned out!

To my Baby Momma Zatasha I love you boo!! And to all the Bookies I appreciate the love and support you show all authors not just me. It makes a *difference having a place where we are respected, celebrated and offered endless support!*

To my friends and family: I appreciate all of the love and support. My cousins, Dionne, Donna & Tanisha. My friends: Letitia, Natasha, Jennifer, Diana and Kia. I'm truly grateful for you all, and I love you. And to my best friend there will never be enough letters in the alphabet to thank you.

To all of my fans, readers, test readers, admins and anyone who has ever read or purchased my work, shared a link or a book cover, you're all appreciated, and I promise to keep pushing on your behalf to write what you're looking for.

Copyright © 2018 by Tina Marie
All Rights Reserved

This book is a work of fiction. Names, characters, places, and incidents either are the product of the author's imagination or are used fictitiously and are not to be construed as real. Any resemblance to actual persons, living or dead, business establishments, events, or locales, is entirely coincidental. No portion of this book may be used or reproduced in any manner whatsoever without written permission except in the case of brief quotations embodied in critical articles and reviews.

Synopsis

Tsunami is faced with one of the toughest decisions of his life. The rules of the streets say you kill those responsible for touching those that belong to you. When the person behind Mya's shooting is revealed, will he be able to pull the trigger?

After being shot, Mya wakes up to learn that her condition is the least of her problems. Her mother has yet again turned her life upside down taking her child and teaming up with an enemy Mya didn't even know she had. Unsure of what to do, Mya tries to get back control of her life but it's proving to be harder than she ever thought.

Lynk, Sarai, Scar and Xanaya are stuck fighting their own battles but everyone's fight seems to revolve around the same thing; Mya's shooting and who is responsible.

Love and boundaries will be tested. Secrets will begin to surface and the silence starts to scream louder than words. Can everyone get their lives back on track after the tragic incident or will the love they shared just not be enough to pull them through?

Table of Contents
Chapter 1- You Just Never Know
Chapter 2- Fighting the Good Fight
Chapter 3- You Hold My Heart
Chapter 4- Take No Prisoners
Chapter 5-Rising above
Chapter 6-Run into Your arms
Chapter 7- Masks off
Chapter 8- Standing on my Own
Chapter 9- Crossing all the Lines
Chapter 10- Damsel in Distress
    Epilogue

Chapter 1 - You just never know

Chania

As soon as I heard the shots I knew my life was over. They were meant for Xanaya not Mya and if she died I would die too. I was going to die from heart break if Tsu didn't kill me first. I loved her like a sister. She was there for me through every set back in my illness and in my life since we became friends. She never treated me like something was wrong with me. I immediately felt the tears begin to roll down my face, hot and sharp. They stung like tiny knifes burning tracks through my skin.

I was stuck, I couldn't move even though everyone around me was moving. My phone was buzzing non-stop and I knew it was him. I wondered if he realized he hit the wrong person. He was crazy, not crazy like gangster crazy I mean crazy like white boy serial killer crazy. I had heard rumors before I got mixed up with him but I looked the other way. Now I wish I wouldn't have, and I knew if for some reason Tsunami didn't kill me he would.

Slowly I managed to stand on wobbly legs so I could go outside and see the damage. I prayed the whole way there that Mya was ok. That she was just shaken up and not lying in a pool of blood on the cold concrete. As my foot hit the last step I realized my prayers had went unanswered. Mya was sprawled out in front of her car that was still parked in her driveway. She had blood pouring from somewhere on her head and her leg. She was perfectly still and all I could hear was Xanaya cursing and Sarai's sobs. Mya had a look of surprise on her face, like she couldn't believe that she was shot. Tsunami looked at me with so much hate in his eyes I thought I was going to melt into a puddle from the fire. He didn't waste any more time on me as he rushed to Mya's side.

FUCK! Yea, my life was over. The look confirmed he knew I had something to do with this even if no one else did. I wondered if he thought I did this to Mya on purpose. I wanted to speak up, to explain, but the explanation wasn't any better. I was going to have someone killed so I could take their man, and her ass was standing right here. And it wasn't like Scar was nicer than Tsunami. In love with him or not he was a scary ass nigga.

I was really starting to have regrets on my reckless plan. Shit a baby would have died because of my desires. I was the monster all along and the fucked up thing was that if Mya didn't get hurt I wouldn't have cared one bit. I would have been pulling my hoe panties on and trying to snatch the man I craved. While everyone was busy fussing over Mya I slid back in the house. I had to get out of there fast before I heard the unthinkable and before Tsunami murdered me. I knew when it came to Mya he wouldn't think twice. She was the only person who ever really mattered to him.

I raced to the couch and grabbed my purse but couldn't find my cell phone anywhere. What the fuck I knew I left it sitting there. I frantically searched my pockets and it wasn't there either. "Looking for something," Scar's deep voice said while he held the phone up. I felt drops of pee leak from my frightened ass pussy. *SHIT*. He wasn't supposed to be in here snooping around. My mind was going a thousand miles a minute trying to figure out should I run or scream or just remain calm. Deciding to try and run I turned as fast as I could ready to jump over the end table and make my way to the kitchen and out the back door.

"Bitch you really thought I was gonna let you make it," Scar asked as he wrapped his arm tight as hell around my neck. I had barely made it two feet before he caught my ass. "You coming with me bitch," he said dragging me to the backyard. He snatched my purse and picked up some clothes line that was lying outside. Before I could blink I was tied up and shoved in his trunk with a dirty ass pair of boxers stuffed in my mouth. I swear his nasty ass had to have fucked in these dirty drawers because they tasted like nut and ass.

I knew I should be thinking of something else, like the way I was going to die. It could have been worse I guess, it could have been Lynk that caught me. I knew he would torture me before all was said and done. Scar might actually rape me or some shit. At least then I could die with a good memory. He left the trunk open and I suddenly heard a females voice.

"I knew that bitch was off, I kept telling Mya to watch her ass. Scar you can't have her to yourself I want in on whatever you have planned for this bitch." Sarai's face appeared at the edge of the trunk, her eyes were intense as she picked up the tire iron that was back here with me. "WHAP," she hit me in the ribs and I cried out as the metal connected. I tried to scoot back in the trunk even with my hands and feet tied but it didn't do much good. Over and over again Sarai hit me and I wondered where everyone else was. Why the hell no one wasn't looking for Scar or Sarai's ass? She was laughing and crying at the same time. I knew that bitch was looney toons. She must have got that shit from her man.

"Scar get in and drive I will follow you," she demanded as the trunk was slammed shut and I was surrounded by darkness. Didn't she have a fucking kid to tend to? Maybe she wouldn't show up and then I would have a chance to get Scar on my side. He wouldn't kill his best friend sister, or would he? I was being rolled around in the trunk like a basketball my head was being bounced off the hard ass metal. I swear it felt like this nigga hit every pot hole in the town. My mind was running a thousand miles a minute trying to figure out some way to get out of whatever I had coming.

Scar

I wished I could say I was surprised at this shit but knowing how fucked up people was in this world I wasn't. Even a sister betraying her brother was like someone telling me the sun rose in the morning. When the shots rang out and everyone's eyes landed on Tsunami mine were trained on Chania ass. I heard her scream out *no* when Mya went outside and that left me curious as to what the fuck she had going on. As soon as the first shot was let off her face turned pale and she had her phone in her face furiously texting someone. Once everyone made their way outside and I noticed her phone got left behind I decided to see who was so important she had to text them right after her friend was shot at.

I sat in the front seat of my car scrolling through the messages in this bitch Chania phone trying to figure out what nigga she was using to have my girl killed. I was startled by a knock on my window. Grabbing my gun I almost bust off on Sarai crazy ass. I didn't even know how the fuck she got in my garage to begin with. She stood there with Mulan on her hips rolling her eyes so hard that shit looked painful. "Nigga I told you I was handling this shit wit you so let's go. Fuck you in here doing writing Xanaya a love letter." She grabbed for the door handle and tried to yank open my shit. Of course Xanaya friend would be fucking crazy too. Sighing I got out of the car, if she wasn't holding the baby I would have whacked her with it for having a slick ass mouth. If Lynk didn't stop hiding on that damn Island and come get this girl I was wrapping her ass up in some bubble wrap and putting her in a Fed Ex box.

"I fucking told you I got this, what you going to do beat her while holding the baby," I said cutting my eyes at her. "Get back in your car and get the fuck on. Go sit at the hospital next to your friend's bedside like any normal female. Out here trying to play super thot and shit. What your bra turn into a weapon" I said walking towards my front door hoping she would get the hint and leave. Instead she was on my fucking heels like a Pitbull. Turning around I stood over her with an annoyed look on my face. "Real talk Sarai get the fuck out of here, you got ten seconds to get off my lawn before I hit the red button on the alarm and the police come get yo ass. This shit got to be all kinds of trespassing and harassment."

"You calling the cops and got a woman tied up in the trunk, Scar open the door and stop playing I have other things to do after this, like go be by my friend's side as you suggested. All I need to know is why she would do this to Mya, especially after all Mya has done for her and then make her ass pay." Opening the door I let her in but left Chania in the trunk. I had to prep the basement before I brought her in. I sat down to finish scrolling through the more recent messages trying to get the details on what this sneaky bitch was up too.

She had almost twenty new messages from a name saved in her phone only as M. The last one made my skin crawl.

M: *We had a fucking deal Chania and you broke the deal. Xanaya will still be mine to punish as I see fit and as for your ass I have plans for you when I see you. You can ignore my calls and texts but I could tell I shot the wrong woman tonight. You tried to play me, you sent out the wrong girl and that's why I shot her. I had no intentions on killing Xanaya yet. No she owes me a lot and I planned on collecting. I still plan on collecting.*

I can fantasize how good she will look finally broken, on her knees begging for my love and forgiveness. As for you, well Chania I will meet you in hell.

Clicking on her pictures next I saw some of Xanaya at her crib, her job and then at Mya's house. Next they were all of me, fuck I was shocked to see me in her phone at all. I was speechless when I saw how many. Thousands of images saved in her IPhone were of my ass. "What the fuck," I said out loud as I scrolled through them. She had pictures of me at the park, the club and even some from when we used to all go to school together. Her crazy ass had been stalking me for years. This was never about Xanaya or Mya, it was about Chania's obsession with me. When she confessed her "love" a while back and tried to hop on my dick I just thought she was doing regular pop off shit. Or that her meds had her head fucked up. I wish I would have taken it more seriously.

From the sounds of M he knew Xanaya and wanted revenge. I sat back and ran my hands over my face. Xanaya was always in some shit, no telling what man she stole money from, fucked they homeboy or just straight crushed they soul. I turned her into an emotionless monster and now someone wanted her to pay. I had to protect her, no question about it. Shit I loved her and she had my shorties. She would always be my fucking girl! I looked up to see Sarai sitting on the edge of the couch with her leg jumping up and down in anticipation. Her eyes were wide open like a crack head waiting on a fix, watching every move I made. "What did you find Scar, I know that's Chania phone. She's the only one with that bright ass phone case." I shook my head hoping she would just shut up.

"Stay here," I warned Sarai as I jogged downstairs. Grabbing a hard metal chair I put it in the middle of the room as I spread sheets of plastic all over the floor. "Grrrr," my Rottweilers Rage and Naya growled letting me know they wanted out of their cages. "Not yet girls, soon," I said and they both laid down looking at me, their eyes filled with anticipation. I knew they eventually would have a lot of fun with Chania. Hearing a thump and a muffled scream I ran upstairs. Of course Sarai was not where the fuck I left her. Mulan was calmly sitting in the playpen I kept for Favour eating a cookie. "Where is yo crazy ass mama at," I asked as I walked back to the garage? She looked up at me with her bright eyes and smiled. Yea even she knew her mama was a damn living nightmare.

"Sarai," I seethed, getting her attention. She stood there with her foot midair ready to crash into Chania's face, again. She had lit into her so bad I was surprised her head was still on her body. "I told you wait for me, you don't fucking listen. Now back up off her ass so I can put her downstairs. Got blood all over my fucking garage and shit I hope you don't care about those clothes because your cleaning this shit up" I bitched as I snatched Chania up and flung her over my shoulder, she grunted as her soft body made contact with my hard one. I swear Sarai was about to get her ass whooped right along with Chania. "Move, what the fuck can I walk," I snapped tripping as Sarai was still sending licks to her head while I was trying to carry her and walk up the stairs.

"Fuck that Scar she's the reason my best friend was shot, I promise I won't stop. I'm dragging this bitch every time I see her face and imma drag your ass too if you get in my way," she said slamming the door as we made it inside. What the fuck I thought her and Mya used to be the calm ones now they both went all Chuckie in this bitch. Once I had her in the chair I tied her hands and feet to the legs and took the opportunity to slap the shit out of her. I wasn't into hitting bitches but just the knowledge that she wanted Xanaya dead made me want to rip her fucking head off. "Scar why are you holding back, just shoot her already. Give me your gun and I will do it." Sarai was looking around the basement, her eyes searching every shelf like I just had weapons lying around for her leisure.

Grabbing Sarai by the arm I shoved her up the stairs making sure to turn out the lights on Chania snake ass. I would deal with her later. "Sarai look, it's time for you to go. I respect your loyalty to Mya, I really do. Hell loyal friends are clearly far and few between. Now I'm not into explaining shit to people but I will give you a few details before you leave. Mya was not the person who was supposed to be shot. This shit aint got nothing to do with her but it did have something to do with Xanaya and you know I can't let that shit slide. I can't just go bust off this girls head for several reasons. The main one is because she has a partner and I needed info from her to find our enemy." Sarai stood there watching me for a few minutes. I guess she was wondering if I was telling the truth or not.

Suddenly all the anger she was holding on to fell away and the tears cascaded down her face. She sank down on my kitchen chair and waved me away when I tried to hand her a paper towel because her nose was leaking like a mother fucker. Crying females really wasn't my specialty. "Ok Scar I'm going to trust you," she got out in between sobs. "Don't make me fuck you and her up Scar. I been peeped her little scrawny ass checking you out a long time ago. I don't know if you bust open that used up pussy or not and I don't care. Just don't allow it to cloud your judgement." Sarai had jumped up and got in my face as she said the last part. Damn I guess I was fucking a lot of bitches in these streets because it looked like that's all everyone thought I was good for.

"Sarai don't tell any fucking body she's here. I need to do shit my way. I can't deal with anyone emotions and she is Tsunami's sister." Shaking her head in agreement she finally wiped her face and got up to grab Mulan. I guess she called herself giving me one final look as she strolled out the door and got in her car. Crazy ass didn't even wipe up all the blood. Picking up the phone I called Xanaya a few times to make sure she was ok but she didn't answer. Fuck I would have to go over there and tell her to be on the lookout. I could just imagine how this conversation was going to go. I didn't want anyone to know I had Chania until I got the info I wanted and decided how she would meet her maker.

    I decided to try and get some rest and deal with the walking dead tomorrow. I took a few shots of Crowne to the head and still couldn't relax. A few bitches hit my line but I honestly didn't want to fuck I wanted to kill. Letting my head fall back and hit the head board with a thud I tried to focus. All I could think about was murdering Xanaya. I had never killed a bitch before but there was always time to try new pursuits. I guess I should get up and give the hoe some water or crackers. I had to keep her alive and this was my first time having a hostage in my home. Sliding my feet into some Jordan slides I stumbled to the kitchen. All those drinks were starting to catch up to my ass. In the middle of the stair case my feet flew out from under me and I landed hard on my back. Laughing into the quiet house I rolled over and slowly stood up. Good thing I didn't have my gun in my waist or I would have shot my damn self.

    All that shit didn't matter though I was still going to drink everything in sight. That's what kept me numb. I didn't have to think about losing Xanaya or Favour, or being stuck with annoying ass Shelly Ann for at least another fifteen years. I drank and the world went black, all the chaos became background noise and I no longer had to care. Looking in my kitchen I grabbed a bottle of water and some toddler cookies. Shit it was all I could find. Making my way downstairs all I could smell was piss and blood. Jesus I was going to have to take this bitch to the bathroom too. I started thinking that killing her ass fast was a better idea. Pulling the rag out of her mouth and untying just her hands I shoved the snacks and water in her hands.

Of course her dumb ass didn't even take the opportunity to eat just start yapping at the mouth. "Scar come on don't do this. You know how much I love you. I did this for us, so we could be together and you didn't have to worry about Xa-." Before she could even get Xanaya's name out of her mouth I had grabbed her by her already injured jaw. The pain caused her to choke on the cookie she was nibbling like this was a fucking meeting at a country club. Roughly I hit her back a few times and got right back in her face. I noticed she didn't have a look of fear in her eyes at all. Well should I say eye because one was completely swollen shut. Sarai did a number on her. I was surprised she could see at all.

Gripping her jaw even tighter before I spoke I made sure to talk slow. I didn't want her to miss a fucking word. "First of all I don't give a fuck who you love. I don't like yo hoe ass, I didn't like you before this. Second of all don't fucking say my girl name, ever. I'm trying my best to keep you alive long enough to get what I need but don't make me say fuck it and just chop of your fucking head." I could see tears streaming from her eyes in a straight line. I didn't know if it was because of the pain I was causing her or because I didn't love her psycho ass back. I pulled up another chair and watched while she ate and drank. Her movements were calm. I guess she thought I wouldn't kill her. But I would. It was always the people who thought they wouldn't get touched that did.

I drummed my fingers on the top of the metal chair I was straddling and began humming some R&B song I heard on the radio. We just sat there looking at each other as time ticked by. "Scar are you waiting on me for something,

I mean shit I'm the one tied up in your cold and dark basement. I'm the one waiting on you to come to your senses and let me go. Or even better you can let me go upstairs and clean up so I can take you to Heaven," she said licking her blood crusted lips. I almost threw up on her. She must have been insane long before today. I exercised patience and let her just keep talking none sense. I aint have shit else to do.

"So you ready to tell me what I want to know? Shit all I want is M's identity and you can make your way to those pearly gates in the sky," I told her. Her face took on a surprised look, I guess she thought a nigga was gonna lie to her and promise she would live. I didn't operate like that. She began laughing as she brought the boxers I used to gag her back up to her mouth were she shoved it in. It was a move of defiance on her end but I was not impressed. Walking over to the utility shelves I had I opened up the nearest box and grabbed a hammer. Walking over to her I took the hammer and raised it above my head. Slamming it down on her knee I could hear the crunching of her bones. She screamed out in pain. Walking to the corner of the room I grabbed a bucket and filled it with all hot water. I made sure to add a little bleach and some Tide. Taking it over to Chania I threw it on her to wash off the stench. I rinsed her in the same hot ass water from head to toe.

She was making silent screams through her makeshift gag and shaking in extreme pain. Smiling I moved next to her and whispered in her ear, "I will get that name." Throwing a thick rough blanket on her I went upstairs to get some rest. I still had the urge to slice her throat and watch her bleed out but my head was banging from the hang over I felt coming on.

Chapter 2 - Fighting the Good Fight

Xanaya

Between this pregnancy and taking care of an extra child on top of mine I had slowed all the way down. Poking my head in the living room I scanned the whole room double checking that the baby gates were in place and only baby friendly toys covered the living room floor. Babies moved fast and I wasn't taking any chances. Pregnant or not I was about to have a glass of wine. Pouring some pink Mascato I grabbed a big ass bag of Cheetos and hoped the kids wouldn't want any, Tamir little grown ass ate everything. Making my way to the couch I gently tossed myself down on the pillows and went in on my snack.

Channel surfing I realized I was lonely. My cousin wouldn't wake up and I haven't spoken to Scar ass since the night of the shooting. It was best to avoid him altogether for now even though I knew I would have to deal with the situation with him and the baby I was carrying eventually. I thought about calling Sarai but Mulan had been fighting a summer cold so she was probably feeling just as stuck as me. I knew we both missed the fuck out of Mya though. It felt like a piece of my heart was ripped out. It had always been me and her and now I honestly didn't even know if she would be ok.

Oddly enough, Chania's ass just went missing ever since the shooting. She never even made her way to see Mya at the hospital or called for an update. I wondered what her problem was, I never liked her hoe ass but she and Mya were super close so something felt off about the situation. I tried to ask Tsunami but he just gave me a rude ass look and ignored my questions.

Fuck him and his sister, nigga stayed with a fucking attitude. If he wouldn't have upset my cousin to begin with she would have been here with me telling me not to drink this Mascato.

Seeing lights flash in the windows I pulled the curtains to the side and squinted as someone's high beams shone from my driveway directly into my eyes. I felt my hands get clammy and my heart race. Ever since Mya was shot I swore someone had been following me. I kept telling myself it wasn't for real and that it was just me being paranoid because of my cousin being hurt. But deep inside I knew some shit wasn't right. For example Saturday I went to the grocery store and every time I turned around I caught a flash of black zoom out of sight.

Focusing on the situation outside, I saw the lights go out suddenly and a dark figure step out of the car. Even though he had on a dark hood I let out a sigh of relief as soon as I saw him walk towards the house. I knew who it was just from the way his bow legs moved in the street light. Opening the door before he could even ring the bell I made sure to put a mug on my face and cross my arms with an attitude.

I snatched open the door before he could lift his hand to knock. I had the words to cuss him out ready but seeing his face left me at a loss. Scar would always be the only man who gave me butterflies, lots of headaches but butterflies too. "Xanaya move the fuck out the way man and let me see my son," he said damn near shoving me to the ground. And just like that he ruined any loving feelings I had towards him. He was already on the floor scooping up Favour and holding him close. "Don't come over here saying shit to me," he barked as I made my way into the room. I could smell the liquor on him from a few feet away.

"So you think you're going to come over here to be around my son drunk? Are you fucking crazy? Nigga it's time for you to leave, as a matter of fact I never even invited you to come in. You always think you running some shit." I walked over and grabbed Favour from him and immediately felt bad when he began screaming and reaching for Scar.

"You know what Xanaya, you are such a bitch how much longer are you going to keep me from my son?" He staggered a little almost tripping on a few of the oversized Legos that the kids were drooling all over. "I love my son," he said slurring his speech. I was too busy trying to calm my son down as he cried uncontrollably for the man he thought was his father. Tamir sensing his cousin's distress also began crying. Lawd, my night of snacks, reality TV and wine had turned into a three ring circus. Deciding I should close my front door I heard the engine in his car still running.

"Fuck," I mumbled as I threw on my house shoes and ran outside to hit the button and turn the car off. I couldn't let Scar drive away in his condition. He still had a place in my heart and I wouldn't be able to live with myself if he killed himself driving drunk. When I came back in he was on the couch laid the fuck out sleep even with the kids still crying. Shaking him until he woke up grunting I picked up Tamir in my other arm and poked Scar until he made his way upstairs. Even drunk he was low key looking around my crib as he climbed the stairs slow as fuck with his ole nosey ass. My arms were starting to hurt carrying both the kids. "Man hurry the fuck up this not no grand tour and shit. You lucky I never sent you on your way to go kill yourself. I just don't want that on my fucking head." He turned to me giving me a look of death. I just rolled my eyes, I may be scared of my shadow these days but I sure as hell wasn't scared of Sciony King fucking Jones. "Sciony go to hell," I said moving around him and quickly making my way to Favour's bedroom.

I lowered the railing on the crib and put both babies inside so I could strip them and change their diapers. As soon as I had them wiped off and in clean footie pajamas Tamir was on his belly fast asleep. Favour of course was still crying and wiggling around in my arms. I swear if I didn't know any better I would think he was Scar's baby because he sure had his fucked up attitude. Walking in my bedroom I was glad this nigga knew enough to take off his street clothes before climbing in my bed. He was half asleep and followed my movement with hooded eyes. I gave in and set Favour on the bed next to him. My traitor son instantly clung to Scar's white tee and laid his tear stained head down on his chest. Scar pulled the baby close and they both closed their eyes.

"Aint this some bullshit," I said out loud as I stripped naked so I could get in the shower. Feeling the hot water hit my back I relaxed and ran my hand over the slight bump in my stomach. I swore I was getting bigger every day and the more I thought about getting rid of my baby the more I knew I just couldn't. It sounded so cliché but having a baby grow inside of you really forms an unbreakable bond. Feeling a draft as the shower curtain was ripped open I felt my heart leap into my throat. "What the fuck Scar, knock or something," I yelled.

"Yo you good, you been in here a long ass time ma? And what the fuck you jumping for," he asked as he took his dick out and started to take a piss. Closing the shower curtain I washed up and got out. He was still in the bathroom, in my space. "My baby got yo ass looking good," he said smirking as he slapped my bare bottom. I pulled the towel from the back of the door hook so hard it broke off. He was bringing me to a place of annoyance I didn't know existed. I swear he breathed down my neck the whole time I dried off, lotioned and then brushed my teeth. For several seconds I thought about jabbing him in the eye with the tooth brush but decided I was too tired to fight his overgrown behind.

"Come here," he said as he pulled me closer to him. I felt his hard on poking me in my thigh as he pulled me closer. I knew my pussy was splish splashing just from his touch but I didn't need that kind of drama in my life. He never even explained the shit with Shelly and his secret love child. I couldn't keep accepting less than I deserved from him. I deserved a man who's not cheating on me or lying to me. Pushing him some I tried to move around him so I could get out of his area. "Ma why you playing and shit, come give me some of my pussy," he said holding on to me tighter as his hand began moving closer to my honey pot.

"Scar this pussy belongs to me I wax it, wash it and keep it tight. I'm not falling into this same fucked up pattern with you again. As a matter of fact you shouldn't even be here. We do the same dumb shit every single time. I feel like a broken record." I slapped his hand away as I paused and looked up to see him gazing directly at me. I guess I had his full attention for the first time in a long time. His hand loosened on my arm a little and his body seemed tense.

"Come on Xa, explain how you feel. What dumb shit we bout to do," he asked bringing his face closer to mine. I could hear the anger mixed with sarcasm in his voice. I could feel his breath on my face as he waited on an answer. Shaking my head I just wanted to go to bed and not open Pandora's Box of feelings. Why couldn't me and this nigga ever just be in the same space without fucking and arguing. I mean damn we argued in clubs, parks, schools, there was no limit to our ratchet behavior and I was wore the fuck out. My body began to shake from the cool air on my bare skin. "Naw you got something to get up off your chest and shit so go for it. I'm a grown ass man so I'm sure I can take it." He narrowed his eyes and looked more evil than usual.

"Ok since you want to push, this is the dumb shit. Me and you, we see each other and argue. Then we fuck and go our separate ways. Every time it's the same thing and every time my heart and my feelings get trampled. At the end of the day I'm still alone, I'm still stuck being a single mom and trying to get over the love of my life who just won't forgive me. But who is willing to fuck me on sight. Honestly I deserve better, I deserve to not be so traumatized from loving you that I use and abuse other men. I deserve real love, care and somebody who's down for me. And you know what Scar you don't deserve this shit either. You deserve a woman you trust and can fall in love with and I'm not her," I couldn't help the tears that spilled out of my eyes. They burned a trail down my cheeks and began dripping on my breasts. Scar didn't say anything just stood there for a while.

"Come put some clothes on before you get sick." He led me to the bedroom and found a pair of shorts and t-shirt for me to put on. Suddenly feeling exhausted from all the emotions I had been going through I sunk into the pillows and rolled onto my side. Scar covered me up like a baby and climbed into bed next to me. He pulled me close to him and kissed the top of my head. For the first time ever me and Scar were in the same bed without having sex. I guess that was something.

The next morning I woke up to him laid out on his back and the sheet barely covering his body. I examined his tatted up chest and wanted to rain kisses all over his body. The sound of the boys in Favour's bedroom saved me from that bad decision. I hoped he would have woken up so he could get the fuck out but as I slid my feet to the floor a loud snore came from him. Sighing quietly I hoped he would at least stay sleep for a while so I didn't have to deal with his bullshit. It was way too early. Getting Tamir and Favour cleaned up I went downstairs to cook breakfast. I had taken a leave from my job since I had to help with Tamir and this pregnancy hadn't been the best. I threw up daily and even felt nauseous as I spoke. I made the boys oatmeal with sides of applesauce. I was staying in today because it was getting cold and I had to study for a test.

Once they were in the highchairs eating I sat nibbling on some toast. The doorbell interrupted me just when I got to the buttery part. Stomping to the door I flung it open without looking outside. Honestly I assumed it was Sarai or Tsunami because not to many people came to my house. "Mar, what are you doing here," I said fumbling with my words. I hadn't spoken to him much the past couple of months because, well honestly I had got what I wanted from his ass and I was done. But if asked I could always use the excuse of my cousin being in a coma.

"Shit I came to check on your ass and I'm glad I did. I see why you haven't been contacting me. I can see what we got going on," he said eyeing my belly. He reached his hand out to settle on my stomach. I cringed inside at his touch and began explaining but he continued on. "Damn pretty you could have just told me what was up, I got you and my lil one all the way. You not gonna need for shit. As a matter of fact you need to just let a nigga move in this bitch." He kept right on going like we had been together for years and was madly in love. Is this what good pussy did to niggas? Made them stupid? How could this be his baby when I hadn't fucked him for at least four months and he always strapped up.

"Look Mar, this not your baby, I'm sorry about that but you know we haven't been together in a while. I knew you had a situation so I wasn't taking us too seriously." His face turned from a smile to a frown and his hand lifted in a threatening manner.

"Yo niggas warned me about you but I didn't listen. Bitch I bet this is my baby you so fucking scandalous and I don't believe shit coming out your mouth. You think you getting rid of me that easy you're fucking mistaken." As he moved closer to me I felt sick to my stomach. Hearing a noise on the stairs behind me I knew shit was about to get a whole lot uglier and fast. "Xanaya you aint nothing but a whore, a bitch that plays niggas for their money," he said almost screaming with spit hitting me in my face.

Feeling my body being pulled back I knew Scar had arrived. "Yo Mar, what's good my dude? I know you not calling my girl a whore. You like your fucking life nigga," Scar said in the coldest voice I ever heard. He was gripping me so tight I knew today was going to be a long one even once Mar punk ass was gone.

I guess Mar thought he was Billy Badass because he was standing there with a smirk on his face and I guess no fear in his heart. "Son you claiming this money hungry, tricking ass bitch," he asked laughing at the end? If Scar didn't hurry and fuck him up I was about to. I had just about enough of his slick ass mouth calling me hoes and tricks. I got his hoe right the fuck here. Involuntarily I moved closer to the door ready to clock his soft ass upside the head but Scar turned and gave me a look.

"Son you made because my girl used yo ass. If she a trick, she my trick remember that. She fucked wit you because she could not because she had to because I make sure her and my kids always straight. Now imma be nice today, this once since I can see your broken heart from the tears in yo fucking eyes. You got four seconds to get the fuck out of here and don't come back." He pulled his nine from somewhere and put it to Mar head. He tried to remain hard and turned around giving Scar his back and made his way to his truck.

Scar shoved me in the house and shut the door. He backed me against the wall and I could feel his heart beating fast. I knew he was mad, I knew him and I could see it in his eyes and feel it with every move he made. His hand lightly circled my neck and made its way to my hair. He tangled his hands in my short curls and pulled my face so we were nose to nose. "Scar I don't need a lecture from big brother, you can just get the fuck on. Oh and like you told Mar, don't come back," I spit out with nothing but a fucked up attitude. I wasn't about to stand here and have him tell me shit about what I was doing and with who. We weren't together. "And for the millionth damn time I don't need you to defend me."

His hand tightened in my hair and he took a deep breath like he was trying not to kill my ass. "I won't be telling you again that I got you, I always got you even when niggas is out here calling you whores and shit. Stop taking these fuck boys money, you don't need them you will always have me. Now you need to get your life together or Favour will be living with me and the next one once you drop him or her. My kids won't grow up any kind of way believe that. I love you but I will always love them more. This shit isn't over, and this Mar shit won't be over either. Shit with niggas in the street never ends that easy. So his blood is on your hands." He turned to walk away letting me slide against the wall.

"So that's the way you handle shit huh Scar. You kill anyone who gets in your way. I guess that's what happened to Nazia, he took your girl so you made sure he paid. Now my son has no father. Fuck you Scar I hate you for that. For everything you have done to me but especially for that, now get the hell out of my house," I yelled at the top of my lungs.

Scar

 In that moment I knew Xanaya was truly convinced of two things, one that I wasn't Favour's father and two that I murdered Nazia. I fast walked my way to where she stood and slapped the shit out of her, something I thought I would never do. She didn't react at all just stood there frozen her hand lightly touching the spot that was already turning bright red on her caramel colored skin. I put on my black Timbs and hurried to my car. I had some unfinished business with Mar and I just wasted precious time arguing with her ass. I was in such a rush I left my hoodie inside but it was cool I had an extra one in the trunk. Throwing it on I jumped in my Maserati and started the car. Checking that my clip was full I slowly and carefully made my way to go and have an impromptu meeting with Mar.

 As I crept through the hood I thought about this shit with me and Xanaya. I never meant for her to find out about Kevon like that. No one even knew me and Shelly had a kid back in the day. I made her keep him a secret because she was a hoe and I didn't want to hurt Xa. Shit I didn't even think the little nigga was even mine but at this point I was all he knew. I had hurt Xa a lot of times and a lot of ways but this was probably the worst. There was no coming back from this shit so I wasn't even going to try anymore, that was why I didn't apologize, she had to be tired of my I'm sorrys. The ironic thing was I had access to a kid that probably wasn't even mine and now I would probably never see my real son again. Yea Favour was my fucking son not Nazia's not anyone else's and so was that baby Xa was carrying right now. I had the DNA test done on Favour months ago just like I said I was. Even though I didn't need it, my grandmother had finally confirmed it for me one day. She was bathing my son and I was staring at him doing the same thing I always did, searching for proof. She looked at me like I was crazy.

"What the fuck you doing looking at him like that," she asked me with a smirk?

I wasn't going to answer her but I just said fuck it. She raised my ass when no one wanted me so there was no way I was lying to her. "Grams I been trying to see something on Favour that looks like me. I know I fucked up with Xa and that's a wrap but I feel like Favour is my son. I just can't figure it out. I been stressing about it since the day he was born." I sat on the edge of the sink with my head in my hands. I looked up when she started laughing at me.

"Scar you always were a hard headed little boy. I don't know how many times I have to keep telling you Xanaya loves you. She never stopped and of course Favour is your son. Come on, come closer." She picked him up and wrapped him in a towel. She turned him over in her arms and showed me his backside. Giving Grams the side eye I was about to walk out. "Look at the birth mark on the inside of his right leg, right there," she pointed to what looked like a heart shaped scar. I hope Xanaya aint let no one hurt my shorty. "All the males in our family have that birth mark, you, Jacobi, even your great granddaddy. Now stop watching my great grand baby and go find something to do like make up with his momma." She shooed me away laughing.

I only got the DNA test because I thought I may have needed it in court someday, if Xa ass decided to get slick and keep my son from me. I guess someday had become today. Grams couldn't even get Xa to answer the phone or bring King over. It had been a while and I missed my fucking son. That was the whole reason I came over last night I just couldn't let another day pass without him. The worst thing was I hadn't even told Grams the real reason this shit got so fucked up, but she knew it was my fault.

I had been avoiding her crib because she and the girls give me dirty looks every time I come around. She didn't know about the little boy I had with Shelly and I slowly felt like everything was crumbling around me.

Pulling up to Goodman Street and looking around I knew I would find Mar's punk ass over this way. He was always at the weed spot sitting outside smoking. I sat back and peeped my surroundings I didn't want my temper to get me caught up some shit I couldn't get out of, like prison. This nigga sat on the step talking to every girl that passed by. Every time one of them rejected him he called them names or threw rocks at they asses. What a fool. Eventually he got up and walked around back, I assumed to take a piss. I hopped out and crept behind him only to find him jerking his dick to a picture of some naked white bitch in his phone. Where in the world these niggas come from, like damn you couldn't do that shit at home?

Putting my chrome to the back of his head I asked the only question I needed to know. "Nigga you ready to die?" I pulled the trigger before he could respond. I didn't give a fuck about a response. Grabbing his phone out his hand before he crashed to the ground I hurried and went through his pockets and snatched his other phone. I guess M got what was coming to him. Now as soon as I confirm it was him working with Chania I could get rid of her ass. Driving to a gas station on Main Street I pulled in and grabbed Chania's confiscated phone from the middle console. I called the nigga M's number and waited for one of this niggas phones to ring.

"So now you fucking decide to call me. Bitch I hope you know you're dead." A voice said on the other end. He sounded, detached from the world, like those serial killers on crime shows. So if this nigga was M, I killed Mar for nothing. Hanging up I hit the steering wheel hard in frustration. Looking down at my stinging hands I still didn't know who the fuck M was.

Chapter 3 - You Hold My Heart

Tsunami

The moment I heard the first shot I thought Mya had gone to the extreme and tried to end it all. I kept going over the image of her face when she ran out of the house. She was beyond hurt and stressed, it was the same look she had when I found her in the hallway bloody and beaten from her mother's hands. She had the look of someone who had given up, on everything. But the screeching of tires and a glimpse of a black F140 as it bent the corner so fast they took out a stop sign told me immediately she didn't do this to herself. Seeing Mya laid out on the ground blood pooling around her caused my heart to stop mid beat. All the breath left my body.

Everyone who was in the house ran out to huddle around her except my mom who kept the kids inside. I cradled Mya's head in my lap, "Mya please don't leave us ma," I begged. I didn't care that I had tears in my eyes. Looking up I guess I was waiting on someone to tell me everything would be alright but all I saw was the same shock and sadness that I felt. Until my eyes landed on my sister, knowing her my whole life caused me to buck at the look on her face. It was one filled with guilt, the same look she wore when she lost our mom's diamond earrings or she broke my game system when she was thirteen.

Of anyone I would have suspected having anything to do with Mya being hurt she was the last person I would have thought. Mya loved her unconditionally and I thought she felt the same. I quickly brought my focus back to the love of my life but I knew that I would have to deal with Chania, sister or not I couldn't let this slide. As soon as the ambulance pulled up and snatched Mya from my arms I jumped up to go with her. Looking at my mother standing on the front porch holding Tamir I stopped Xanaya from getting in her car. "Go get my son and keep him, please. I can't trust anyone else. Don't let him go with anyone else, not even my mom," I knew the seriousness in my voice had her paying close attention.

I stood there waiting until she had Tamir in her arms and my mother was leaving. She was talking shit and cussing me out but I aint have time for any of that shit. She could talk to her damn self. I wasn't interested in talking to anyone but the fucking doctors who were going to save my girls life.

***

Sitting in the hospital room looking at Mya I let my head drop in my hand. I couldn't think about anything but her waking up at the moment. I knew the rest would come soon enough. The revenge, getting to the bottom of the motive and the rage I would feel. I pushed it all to the back of my mind so I could put all my energy into Mya. Stroking her hair away from her head I closed my eyes and started praying. I couldn't lose her, she was my world. I knew I had fucked up on so many levels. It's crazy that it takes a tragedy to realize what you should have been doing the whole time. How you should have treated someone and all the shit you could have done differently but didn't. That was me I had more regrets than I could count.

I thought about all the times she casually mentioned wanting to speak to someone about all she had been through. And how I brushed it off assuming she would eventually get over it. I was insensitive, I didn't take her pain seriously and I had a mouth full of apologies ready. But it had been three weeks and still nothing. She was lying there so still, hooked up to monitors, eyes still closed. My head shot up as the door opened and Scar stepped in. I had already sent Xanaya home with Tamir for the day so I was glad they didn't run into each other.

I wanted to talk to Scar about getting eyes on my sister because she had been missing since the day of the shooting. My mother stopped by yesterday crying about how she hadn't come home in weeks. Shit I didn't feel bad at all I just hoped her sneaky ass hadn't ran off somewhere before I could fuck her up. Shit I saw Chania's face when she came outside, she looked like she had saw a ghost. Her sneaky ass was up to something. Lately her behavior had been all bad. She thought going to a city an hour away and fucking random guys and bitches wouldn't get back to me.

"Yo, she woke up yet," Scar asked as he moved further into the room? I just shook my head not even bothering to respond. The doctors had removed a bullet from Mya's left thigh and her lower abdomen. Thankfully our baby, the one she didn't want was ok. She was blacked out now from a bullet that grazed her head. Honestly I thought she just didn't want to wake up and deal with all the drama going on around her. She was hiding from the world. I wish I could go somewhere and hide too shit. But I was a man and that wasn't an option, ever.

"You know Mya's gonna be aight, she's the strongest girl I know." Scar spoke as he pulled up a chair and threw himself in it. He had welts on his neck and I wondered if he had a run in with Xanaya today. I could see her scratching the shit out of him. "You ok," he said his voice trailing off as he glanced at Mya lying there as like a corpse?

I didn't know how to feel or how I was doing. My feelings of regret had turned to feelings of frustration just that fast. Not just with the whole situation right now but with all the shit Mya and I went through in our relationship. "Look it's not that easy son. Yea she's gonna wake up but then what. She wants to kill our baby, what the fuck am I going to do with that? How can I forgive her for certain things and find a way for us to be together? Hell is she going to forgive me for all the stuff I did. It's all up in the air." I meant that shit, for the first time ever I didn't see a future with me and Mya. Since the first day I saw her and we was just some snotty nosed ass kids I knew she was the one. My forever girl and I always thought that no matter what I did she would be there waiting when I was ready. I didn't count on any of the shit happening that did.

"Nigga you tripping come outside and hit this fucking blunt. Your mind aint right but I get it. Your girl is laid up in this hospital fucked up. You and Mya are what real love is all about. You just in your feelings right now, all this shit going to work itself out."

"You don't understand. I gave up everything for Mya and it's like she never trusted me. Like all I did never meant shit to me. She wants to kill my seed, I can't be ok with that shit. She always make shit seem like it's all me. I moved out the townhouse because I asked her ass to marry me and she turned me down. I wasn't even mad, I can't even lie she had a real nigga heart hurting like a mutha. She's young so I tried to brush that shit off but it still gets to me. I'm here trying to keep my mind on just wanting her to wake up but shit I want it all. I want her to wake up and want our baby and want her to be mine." I could hear the anger in my voice but fuck it that was all I had left was anger.

After that we just sat in silence until Scar got up to leave. I took his advice and went outside to his car to smoke some fire shit. He offered me the bottle of Henny and I declined. Lately he had been drinking himself into a daily coma. I wasn't going for the drunk look, that shit wasn't cute and it wasn't good for business. Right now I had enough problems in my world. I went back in the sterile hospital room and settled in to the hard ass recliner they put next to Mya's bed. Running my hand over hers I knew I would never be able to fully leave her alone. I guess Scar was right the love I had for her was unimaginable to most and unbreakable to me.

"Da da da," I woke up the next day with a crick in my

neck from sleeping in the recliner by Tamir calling out to me as Xanaya settled him and Favour in the room.

"Come on Mya enough of the bullshit, I'm pregnant and I need you. So wake up already. The doctor said we are just waiting on you so let's go. Tsunami needs a shave, and a shower but this nigga won't leave until your eyes open so hurry up." She was stroking Mya's face as she kept talking to her. "Tsu she is going to wake up soon and then we can whoop her ass for making us worry." She gave me sisterly hug as she sat down and stretched out her legs in front of her.

Playing with Tamir I kissed him on his fat cheeks and bounced him on my legs. He giggled and shrieked. Being a baby was easy, shit as long as they got food and attention all was right in their world. "Xa I appreciate you and Sarai taking care of Tamir for me. I can't be taking care of him and being her for Mya at the same time." Someone knocked on the door but before I could call out for them to come in it flew open with so much force it hit the wall behind us.

"There's my grandson with that monster, go get him," demanded Mya's mother as she strolled in with two police officers and that bitch ass nigga Haze behind her. She reached for Tamir and I stood up moving my son closer to me. He clung on to my neck like he knew something wasn't right.

"Bitch you know you not taking my son any fucking were. Why would I allow you to have anything to do with him? Officers please remove this person from the premisise," I spat. If the cops weren't all over the room I would have shot her ass. She looked worse than the last we saw her and I wondered where she had been hiding at. Her eyes were sunken in and she had lost a ton of weight. I wondered if she was doing more than just drinking.

"Sir we are going to ask that you hand over the child in question a Tamir Merrick to his maternal grandmother. She has informed us that you are the cause of his mother being in the hospital and that the child is not yours but in fact her dead fiancés baby. We have a restraining order that states you cannot be within fifty feet of a Kahmya Davis or Tamir Merrick." The cops went for Tamir and I punched him in his face. My son was snatched from me and began screaming. "Sir again we need you to leave right away."

"Yo this is some bullshit, I would never hurt Mya and she knows that. She was the one who hurt her, almost killed my son while she was pregnant. Tamir is my son, he has my last name and I'm listed as the father on his birth certificate. How the fuck can you just take my damn son." I started shoving the chair and the table so they crashed against the wall. I was enraged the system was so fucked up. How could they just come and snatch a kid from his father.

"If you don't calm down you will be arrested. This is not something we can handle so you will have to contact a lawyer and take this up in family court. Come on so we can walk you out," the bald headed officer said as he grabbed for my arm. I snatched away and walked towards the door. Looking back Xanaya was standing there with tears in her eyes. I gave her a knowing look so watch out for Mya and our baby as best she could. Seeing Kimora holding a sobbing Tamir pissed me off beyond anything. Bitch ass Haze winked at me as he grabbed my son from his grandmother. Breaking the hold mister fuckboy cop had on my arm I snatched Tamir from him. Comforting my son I whispered "I love you" in his ear as I handed him to Kimora and was drug out of the room by two of the uniformed officers.

Mya

I woke up surrounded by darkness, trying to roll over I felt a little bit of pain and something metal. That made me sit right up, this bed was way too small to be my own and uncomfortable. "Tsunami," I called out but no one answered. Feeling something tugging at my arm I looked down and saw the IV. I knew what that meant, that I was in a hospital yet again. That's when I remembered the baby, the one I told Tsunami I didn't want. My hand swept over my stomach and everything seemed ok, no cuts or pain there. Pressing the call button several times I became anxious that it took so long for anyone to come.

By the time the nurse slow walked her ass in the room I was almost having a panic attack. "Why am I in here and where are my boyfriend and my son?" I questioned with an attitude. She rolled her eyes as she smacked on her gum and shrugged her shoulders. Her short bob was cute but her face was not. She was a cross between Ru Paul and Snoop Dog. Seeing I was getting nowhere fast I figured I would ask something she may be able to help with. "Since you don't know shit can you get a doctor?" She threw down the blanket she was folding and huffed her way out of my room. Checking the bedside table for my phone I didn't see it there so I grabbed the phone the hospital had. Dialing Tsunami first it just rang and rang so I left a voicemail.

"Tsunami I'm in the hospital and you're not here, where are you and where is Tamir? I can't find my cell phone so just get up here." I set the phone back in the cradle and ran my hand over my head. Stopping when I felt stitches I wondered if I fell and hit my head. It would be just like my ass to fall down some stairs.

"Well I see you are finally awake Miss Davis, how do you feel?" The old white man who I assumed was my doctor asked me as he flipped open the chart and muttered to himself?"

"Is my baby ok," I asked with urgency in my voice?

"Yes you are ten weeks along now and the baby has been doing fine, strong heart beat and such despite the shooting."

"Shooting? I was shot? I don't remember any of that. I left my house to get some fresh air and that was all I can remember. Where's my son and my boyfriend? They weren't injured were they?" Tsunami must have gotten shot too that's why he wasn't with me. I couldn't think of another reason why he wouldn't be. The room door crept open and a face that I wasn't interested in seeing right now.

"Well your son is fine since he has been visiting and as you can see your boyfriend is alive and well. Maybe he can fill in some of the blanks on what happened to land you in this position. Also you should be able to go home in a few days as soon as we run some tests and make sure you are ok," he smiled as he walked out off to see his next patient.

"Haze where is my son and my phone? Why are you here," I asked with some bitch in my voice. I was not in the mood for this joker and I didn't even know how this nigga knew I was in the hospital. Fuck did I even provide him with a last name. Ole stalking ass nigga.

"Tamir is with your mom, she took over his care once she got the restraining order put in place for Tsunami to stay the fuck from up here. I have been looking out for Tamir though so you don't have to worry." I didn't wait to hear shit else. I jumped out of bed and snatched the IV out of my arm. Blood was leaking like crazy but I didn't even give a fuck. My son was in the hands of my enemy. What the hell happened while I was out of it?

"Babe what the fuck, come on now you got blood squirting all over the place and you look like your about to pass out. I know about the baby and I know it aint mine but its cool ma. Mistakes happen and I'm willing to rock wit you. Now get back in the bed and relax." He tried to lead me back to the bed but I shoved him as hard as I could. Searching the little cupboards and shit I finally found a pink bag with personal belongings in them. I guess because I was shot my clothes didn't make it. All that was there was my cell phone and the locket that Tsunami gave me for my birthday a few years ago. I grabbed both and looked around the room for something to put on.

Not finding anything I powered my phone on and clicked on Xanaya's name. I knew she would come and get me. She answered while shrieking in my ear. "MYA, I'm so glad you're awake finally. I have been coming to see you every day. Don't move I'm on the way up there now."

"Xa hurry, my mom has Tamir and I have to get him right away before she hurts him. And why isn't Tsunami here with me. He should be here. I have no clothes and I can't find my purse. I got to get to Tamir. Can you just go pick him up and bring him with you," I was panicking my heart racing as I leaned against a chair in the room. Losing so much blood was making me dizzy and I thought I was going to faint. Haze came over to help me and I felt sick just having him close. He wasn't the man I needed right now.

The nurse and doctor came in after Haze told them I was bleeding and dizzy. "Miss Davis you have to stay in the bed or I will have to give you a sedative to calm you down." I nodded not bothering to explain shit to these people. I would wait until Xanaya got here then I could get dressed and discharge myself against doctors' orders. I sat there watching the clock and calling and texting Tsunami who was not answering me.

"Haze you can leave and when I can I will call you. I

appreciate you being here for me and wanting to help with the new baby and all I really do. I just have to deal with my situation on my own. I have to figure out what the hell happened to me and get to my son immediately he is not safe with my mother." He looked at me like I was crazy as fuck and shook his head.

"Bae come on now Tamir is fine. That's your mother how can you not trust her? About who shot you I don't really know how to say this but it was that bitch nigga Tsunami that did this to you." He gave me a sympathetic look. I bust out laughing even though my situation was fucked up I laughed my ass off. This nigga was fanciful as hell. Now Tsunami shot me? Yea ok.

"Now you got to go for real. Tsunami didn't shoot me. I'm not even entertaining your foolishness. You're straight trying to get over on me and I don't appreciate it all." He opened his mouth to speak and I picked up the water from my bedside table and threw it right at him. "Nigga leave, I didn't stutter. I tried to be nice then you come in here with some fuckery about my best friend shooting me. I'm so over this shit. GO," I screamed at the top of my lungs.

He turned to leave. "You're a crazy bitch for real, but you gonna be calling me soon enough once you find out the truth." He smirked on the way out.

I was so happy Xanaya came in right after. She came over and gave me a tight ass hug. "Yo Xa I can't breathe," I said laughing a little. "I brought you a sweat suit and some clean underclothes. First thing you need to do is call the cops to remove the restraining order on Tsunami. That's why he wasn't here when you woke up. He was here the whole time and then Aunt Kimora came with the police and said he was the reason you were in the hospital and she feared for you and Tamir's safety. I tried to tell them it was crazy. We still don't know who shot you, but no one would listen. I tried to ask her could I take the baby with me so she didn't have to worry but she insisted on keeping him. I'm so sorry cuz, I really tried."

I hugged her again and told her it wasn't her fault. I knew she would have tried as hard as she could to fight for my baby. My mother was just a slick bitch. I went to shower so she could call the police and I could take care of that. Xanaya's phone had rang a few times before she actually answered it but when she did her face turned pale. "When did this happen? How? His mother is awake and we will be there right away. I don't even want to know why his father wasn't called. Listen the DNA determined that is his father so there was no reason he wasn't called. Stupid mother fucker," she hung up jabbing the red end button.

"What's wrong with Tamir," I asked panic in my voice? I didn't even take time to address the fact that she confirmed Tsunami went ahead and did a DNA test on our son. I didn't have time to feel the joy I knew I should finally knowing the truth, Knowing that Creek did not father my precious baby boy.

"Let's go, Tamir was hurt, his arm is fractured. He's in this hospital downstairs in the pediatric E.R." I jumped up as fast as I could, wincing with the slight pain I felt in my leg. Walking was slow due to the fact that I had been lying in the bed for God knows how long. "Oh I have your purse with me in case you need ID. Oh and I sent a message to Tsunami letting him know to get up here."

Making my way downstairs I was so happy to see my baby. He was lying on his side drowsy from whatever medicine they gave him. He had a thick white cast on his left arm. Seeing that pissed me off to the max. "Hello I'm his mother and I need to know what the hell is going on with my son," I said to the nurse who poked her head in the room. At least the nurses working with children looked a little more competent then the one I got.

"Hello mom, he was in the care of his grandmother and she stated to us that he fell off the bed and wouldn't stop screaming. However the police have taken her for questioning because this does not match up with what the doctor has found. I will let him come in and explain the details." She must have saw how upset I was because she put her hand on my back in a comforting gesture. "Ma'am I'm sure he will be fine. We took x-rays and checked his head for any trauma and none was found. He was alert and speaking when he got here."

"Thank You," I said feeling a little bit of relief. Tsunami appeared at the curtain with the look of death on his face. He damn near shoved me to the side getting to Tamir. "Well hello Tsunami, I'm fine thanks for caring. As you can see I woke up. I'm alive." I said with an attitude.

He turned his cold eyes on me. "I can see you are awake. Good for you. Didn't you notice our son was hurt by your mother," he said it like the shit was my fault. I was in a fucking coma or some shit.

"Yea I can see that because I'm standing here with our child. Why weren't you with him? Or with me when I woke up? I needed you?" I was crying openly at this point. I sat on the end of the bed and held my baby in my arms rocking him back and forth. I had never fought with Tsunami we never had that kind of relationship even when one of us didn't agree. What was happening?

He walked closer to me and pulled me to him. I knew he was still pissed, shit so was I. If I was near my mother I would be whooping the shit out of her. "I should have been there. I would have but I couldn't be. I couldn't get to Tamir because I had to wait on the courts. Since this is child abuse and I have the DNA test results my lawyer said I should easily be granted temporary custody and he can be removed from your mothers care." I nodded into his chest. I just wanted to go home with him and our son.

Chapter 4 - Take no Prisoners

M

    Slamming the phone down on my work bench it shattered into thousands of glass pieces. This bitch Chania got the whole plan fucked up. I knew she was a hoe but I thought she was at least fucking smart. I was so enraged when I saw her send Mya outside and not Xanaya. I had the rope, duct tape and gorilla glue in the trunk waiting on her ass and out comes her cousin instead. That voice in my head became my flight or fight navigator and told my ass to fight. I stayed in the car and shot at her until I saw her hit the ground with blood pouring from her head. I sped away so fast not because I cared if I was caught but because of my rage. After I bent a few blocks I ended up hitting a pretty blonde who was crossing the street. Woopsy. She was now a guest in my basement holdings, tucked away all cozy on the special bed I kept down there. Once I had Xanaya I could finish with this one. Her name was Penny. I would moan her name while I watched her suffer. It really did something to my sex drive watching the girls I chose feel immense pain. Watching as they gagged on their vomit because the pain I caused them was unbearable.

    The call today was really unexpected and had

thrown me off schedule. I couldn't believe Chania had enough nerve to call me at all after the way she fucked up. Sitting back in the all black Chevy Impala I kept just for these occasions I smiled as I watched Scar grabbed Mar. I bet him and Xanaya would feel extra safe now that Mar was dead. They thought that was who shot Mya and got away. Little did Xanaya know I was coming for her, not today but soon. I was actually enjoying the chase more than I thought I would. I hadn't slept in seventy two hours because I has been so busy watching Xanaya's every move. I was a pro at this shit and once I finally did get her it will be so sweet. Like a hunter waiting on his kill, then later enjoying it as a meal.

    I was so happy when I was with Xanaya, her pussy was the best and she was so fucking pretty. I never had any intentions on killing her like the others. But then she decided she didn't need me anymore. Talked to me like some fuck boy. And that nigga Scar, he would get his too. Once I got my hands on his girl and his kid he would regret what he did to me. That day on Hudson when he beat me bloody I ended up with seven missing teeth and a fractured skull. I was walking around looking like a damn freak until I could afford to get my grill fixed. It set me back for months. I didn't get to grab any women during that time frame. I was in too much pain. But now all the pain would be on Scar. I laughed so loud people walking by the car began looking at me but I just couldn't stop.

Chania

I had been in this basement for a few weeks now. I was so hungry I could feel my stomach eating itself. I swear this careless ass nigga Scar barely remembered to feed me every few days. He was too busy fucking a million bitches. The only thing that made me happy about that was none of these hoes were Xanaya so they could have at it until he wifed me. I knew he would eventually come around especially since Mya had lived. I could hear his conversations some times when he stood under the vents. A few days ago he let Sarai come over and torture me some. I was sure he taught her the art of waterboarding. Each time she poured the water over my covered face she would giggle like a little girl getting a new toy. He tried all he could to get me to tell him who M was but I didn't budge. Not because I was worried about his safety but because I was worried about mine. Once he knew who to kill I wouldn't be needed anymore. He had to realize he loved me first.

Hearing heavy footsteps on the stairs my dirty ass pussy began to drip and I got excited. The bright ass lights hurt my eyes and his dogs began going crazy. "Not yet girls," he reassured them like he did every time. I swear those two big mother fuckers was looking at me like a snack. He walked closer to me and slapped the fuck out the back of my head. Damn I swear he was some kind of women beater in an alternate world. I still wanted his ass though. "You ready to tell me who the fuck M is. I been killing every person I can find with a name that starts with M and still have come up with nothing and now I'm getting pissed. This is wasted time. I have better shit I could be doing like fucking bitches or chilling with my kids."

I could tell his patience with me was getting short and knowing who M was probably wasn't going to save me very much longer. I shook my head knowing I couldn't tell. Either way my life was going to be over and I had to be careful to not let that happen. If I had to play some crazy ass game then so be it. I was playing all day. "Maybe if you talked to a bitch nicer I would have more information. Shit I'm trynna be your rida not your enemy. Maybe you can let me get a shower and some good food. Then I can suck your dick real good and I can help you out with the info." I put the best smile on my face that I could.

He laughed so hard I could see all the teeth in his mouth, platinum and otherwise. My smile turned to a frown. "Well fuck you then nigga, I aint telling you shit." I shot at him with an attitude. At this point I really didn't have anything to lose so I might as well get live in this mother fucker. I loved Scar but he was clearly incapable of receiving or giving love back. Clucking my tongue I shook my head like I was talking to a slow ass child.

"Ok cool, I aint bought to lie to you. You won't be getting no fucking shower, home cooked meals or my dick. Now tell me or I kill you. Those are your fucking choices. Your time is running out, tick mother fucking tock." He said in a sarcastic tone as he went to let his dogs out of the cage. Screeching I jumped in my chair but didn't get very far because of my restraints. Those big motherfuckers came and began sniffing around nipping my feet. Great I was going to be eaten alive by big ass Rottweilers. "Oh yea, M said he killing you on sight. Have a good one Chania," he said laughing as he jogged up the stairs.

Chapter 5 - Rising Above

Sarai

Hearing the alarm go off I groaned as I realized it was still dark outside. Six AM came fast but no matter how badly I wanted to roll over in my bed and go back to sleep I hit snooze and jumped out of bed. After losing everything and then breaking down I realized I had to get my life together. Not just for Mulan but for myself. I was happy for the help Lynk gave me but I knew it wasn't a guaranteed forever, and I valued my independence. I was still in love with him but I had to learn to love myself and that was just what I was doing. If someday me and Lynk were meant to be together then we would be. Throwing on my neon green sports bra and black and neon green stretch capris I ran down the stairs. Going to the basement I placed my phone in the docking station and smiled when Bruno Mars sexy voice came blasting through the speakers.

I'll rent a beach house in Miami
Wake up with no jammies (Nope)
Lobster tail for dinner
Julio serve that scampi (Julio!)
You got it if you want it
Got, got it if you want it
Said you got it if you want it
Take my wallet if you want it now

Climbing on the tread mill I began my two mile morning jog, it was an indoor run because Mulan was still asleep but just as good. I found that exercising, especially running wasn't just good for my body it was good for my stress level. I could feel the stress melting away as the sweat rolled down my forehead. I found comfort in my new routine as I hurried and took a steaming hot shower. I got out still humming *that's what I like.* I checked my phone hoping for one of the random texts I would get from Lynk where he asked about Mulan. Shrugging when I didn't see anything except an alert from CNN I shrugged and went to make breakfast. While whipping up some pancake batter I sat back to reflect on all I had been through in my short life. I was content with the fact that it did nothing but make me stronger.

A few weeks ago I went to see a counselor to start dealing with my past. I didn't want to carry all I had been through into my relationship with my daughter. Mulan deserved the best I could give her and since Fabian was just a name on a piece of paper my role in her life carried double the importance. Going through the memories of my mother and sisters was painful at first. But I was learning to take the good and leave the bad. I knew my mother loved me and would be proud of me if she was still alive. That had to be enough for now because it was all I had. The guilt I was carrying around all those years was stupid. My counselor helped me see that I was only a child and couldn't stop a grown man. I still have dreams about that night, my mind creating different scenarios so we all lived.

I had yet to find a way to forgive my father for taking my family from me and maybe I never would, but at least I could forgive myself. I took my time with my aunt and uncle as a lesson learned. What I went through with them helped me realize my biggest fear. Dying and leaving my child to be somehow mistreated by whoever got her. If something happened to me now Mulan could end up with my aunt and uncle or her father and his girlfriend and be stuck in a fucked up situation just like I was. I mean truly no one could take care of her the way I do but at least I had people. Xanaya and Mya would love my daughter like their own. She wouldn't ever be alone or abused the way I was and that helped me to move past my fears.

I cut up my babies pancakes up and went to get her ready. We had a lot to do today because I was starting school in January. I had to drive out to Suny Brockport and get my books. Then I wanted to stop at the toy store and get Mulan some stuff. Since the fire we had to buy almost everything over again. "Good morning mommies Mu Mu," I said as I picked her up from the crib. At eighteen months Mulan was all over the place, running, jumping and almost causing me to have a heart attack some of the time. After wiping her up I put on a pair of blue jean jeggings and a black hoodie from Old Navy. Her black baby Uggs matched perfectly. I brushed her hair up into two ponytails and threw some black and pink bobos in.

Sitting her on the floor once I got downstairs so I could pour some juice I kept one eye on her. "Dada Dada," she said walking around the living room holding a picture frame with an image of her and Lynk. I tried to grab the frame from her and she began having a fit. I swear this little girl was something else.

"Come on give it to mommy and I will call daddy," I said trying to convince her. But she really wasn't old enough to understand bribery. Picking up my phone and hitting the facetime button I clocked on Lynks name. As soon as he answered I held the phone up in front of her not even bothering to let him see my face.

"Daddy's girl what's up," he asked and she squealed and clapped her hands. "You being good for mommy," he said like she was about to answer him for real. He talked to her for a while telling her about all the stuff he was buying her for Christmas and all the pretty birds that were on the island. She didn't get bored at all, just sat there shoving pancakes in her mouth hanging on his every word. I ate my food with one hand while holding the phone with the other. Looking up at the clock above the stove I realized that we had to leave before the book store closed. Plus my fucking hand was getting numb.

"Tell daddy bye bye," I coached her. She waved her sticky hands bye and blew an even messier kiss.

"Sarai," he called out my name right before I could hang up on him. Turning the phone towards me I raised my eyebrows silently asking him what's up. "Man why you running me off the phone wit my babygirl. You foul as fuck ma," he said talking shit. He looked sexy with his shirt off leaning back on his bed. I could see his tatted up chest and the way his top lip curled into a scowl, that shit had me turned on.

"Lynk I got shit to do and holding a damn IPhone up so she can listen to you talk for hours isn't on the list." I was proud of myself for not explaining where I was going and what I was doing. He said he wanted space so he was getting it. I propped the phone up on the cookie jar so I could wipe Mulan off. After a few minutes I noticed he was quiet. Turning to look I thought he had hung up but instead he was just watching us. His blue eye looked stormy and his green eye was brighter than usual.

"Sarai you looking good shorty," he said licking his lips. I winked and made sure to make my ass jump in my skin tight sweats as I turned around. "Yea ok I see you, you trynna get fucked or get fucked up," he asked laughing at his his own dumb ass question?

"Neither," I responded pressing the end button. I hurried and left the house speeding down the I490 to make it where I needed to be. The school parking lot was a zoo when I pulled up and Mulan had fallen asleep like she always did in the car. Rolling my eyes I grabbed the stroller out the trunk and put her in it. Covering her with a blanket I rolled through the light dusting of snow to the main building. The line was out the fucking door just like I thought. When it as my turn I pulled out my schedule and gathered everything I needed. I was majoring in Social Work so I could help kids who were in messed up situations, like I was. I know it wasn't my original plan but I was happy with my choice.

Making my way to Toys R Us I woke Mulan up so she could sit in the cart. She was so excited by all the toys, especially the ones that made noise she was good. I grabbed a bunch of learning stuff, a smart doll house for toddlers and one of those life size plastic houses for her play room. I hope that shit fit in the car. It was normally for outside but it was winter so she could slide and crawl around it in doors. Almost running into another cart from someone who wasn't paying attention I slit my eyes ready to cuss they asses out. "Wow, should a baby be playing on a slide. She's just a baby," commented Fabians, whatever she was.

"No hun that's why we are going for custody. Once she is with us she will be safe," Fabian told her with a smile. Laughing out loud I tried to move around them but before I could I was being blocked in. "Can I speak to my daughter. She needs to be getting used to me anyway for when I have her to myself."

Thinking back to the last time I had fought this old retarded ass nigga in front of my child I decided to make a better choice. I ignored his custody threats because the lawyer Lynk hired me assured me he was no threat. He had a few domestic violence charges on his record and no judge was handing him a kid. The court date was coming up in the New Year but for now I was trying to not show my ass.

Backing down the aisle I made a right and ended up surrounded by kitchen sets. Lawd I could see by the look in Mulan's eyes we were somehow shoving one of these in a cart as well. Grabbing one that made real sizzle noises off the shelf I began dragging it across the ground with one arm while I pushed the cart with the other. Ok I guess I had to call for help. Shooting Xanaya a text asking if she could come meet me she said she was sleeping but Scar was coming with his truck. After checking out I waited in the front for him to pull up. He could put all this stuff in his truck so I didn't have to carry anything. He double parked and came inside rolling his eyes and shit. "Damn ma you bought the whole fucking store or something," he said grabbing he biggest box first. I laughed as I gathered some of the bags to help.

"Girl its cold, give me Mulan and pull your car up." He took the baby out of my arms and she started hitting him with her little mittens laughing. "Ok hit me now while you can little mama. When you get older imma whoop that ass." Me and Mulan looked at him like yea right. Suddenly I felt my arm being violently snatched. Whipping around there was bull dog looking ass Fabian with a snarl on his face.

"So now my daughter is around another nigga? What happened to the one with the fucking crazy eyes? You a real fucking hoe man." He was still gripping my arm. Using my free arm I snuffed his muscular ass in the throat. He backed up choking, his eyes tearing up.

Before he could react Scar had moved in front of me. "Nigga it's time for you to go, now, and I would move fast while you still have a chance." He lifted his hoodie displaying two black nines. Fabia scrambled to grab his girls hand and rush out. Turning to me Scar had this look on his face. I knew I would be hearing from Lynk sooner than later. I rushed out to grab my car too embarrassed to explain my fucked up situation to Scar. His mouth was fly and aint no telling the dumb shit he would say. These were the days I wished I could just grab my kid and move away.

Throwing the car into park I grabbed Mulan and then helped load up the Yukon he was driving. The whole ride to my house I thought about how much I missed Lynk. He was the person I used to talk to about everything, and more than anything else I was missing that. I was so into my feelings I almost missed my exit and had to slam my breaks on and jump in front of a few cars. *Shit.* Leaning back I made sure Mulan was ok and she was in her car seat chewing on some plastic car that most likely belonged to Tamir or Favour. I smiled thinking how grateful I was that I had friends that were more like family.

Pulling into the driveway I let Scar park closest to the door. "This her Christmas shit or what," he said carrying everything inside? Shaking my head no I gave him a smirk. "Man Lynk got ya'll asses spoiled as hell." He was shaking his head like he didn't do the same with his son.

"Boy bye, I saw that toy Ferrari you got little King, he's gonna be terrible when he gets older. Hell he terrible now," I said fucking with him. I knew he was Favour dad the minute that little boy was born mugging all of us.

"Sarai for real you good ma? That nigga be fucking with you," he asked with a worried look on his face.

"Scar thank you, I'm good now go home." I gave him a brotherly hug and walked him to the door. "Tell Uncle Scar later," I coached Mulan. She stood there waving her hands. My baby was always happy. Seeing my phone ring and Xa face pop up on the screen I knew her snitching ass man told her about Fabian.

Lynk

I was finally feeling somewhat at peace since I had made the decision to let Sarai go until I got the call about Mya. I knew my little nigga was hurting and after the shit Scar found in Chania phone the unknown enemy behind all of this shit had to be taken care of. I knew soon enough I would have to go and help my little niggas out. They had become like family to me, Scar even came to Trinidad a dew times to chill. He was a bit wild with the females something about the accents turning him out but it was nice to have company for once. I wondered if the peace I was feeling would last. Seeing my phone ring and Scar's name pop up I had a feeling it wouldn't.

Looking down at the phone I thought about the shit that Scar just told me and ran my hands over my waves. I was pissed but proud of how Sarai handled shit. She didn't get messy. I have been watching her the past few months from a distance and she has really been growing up. I always knew she was a good girl she just had to figure it out. Shit her being a good girl, one I loved was the reason I stayed away from her. But if Fabian thought me not being there meant his ass couldn't get touched he was dead ass wrong. Putting in a call to my uncle I waited until he came on the line. All I heard was straight sex sounds as he banged some bitches back out.

"Really Unc, I'm stuck running all this shit and you over there getting some good pussy," I said laughing as his old ass stopped trying to catch his breath.

"Youngin get you some bad bitches over there. I aint

stopping your flow shit. Now hurry up with what you want because I got two baddies over here waiting for me with nothing on but a sheet." Trying to get the image of my uncle old wrinkled ass fucking young girls out my head I cringed.

"Yo someone fucking with my little shorty and since I can't be there to handle that shit you got to have it taken care of. I will have one of the boys bring you the details and I want this shit handled ASAP. I can't rest if I don't know she good," made sure my voice was cold so he knew I wasn't playing around. He was about that drug shit but didn't know about this killer I got running through my veins.

"Are you talking about that little brown thing that used to come in here with her aunt and uncle? I didn't know you still spoke to her ass. I heard she got around a lot. Maybe this just some shit she brought on herself. You don't need any distractions right now son. I think this should be let go." I shook my head in a slow motion even though I knew that he couldn't see me. Steepling my fingers I became thoughtful. I guess there were a couple of things I had to handle when I got back to the states.

"Hey Pastor, I wasn't asking what the fuck you thought. I was telling you what I need done. If you can't do it tell me so I can come handle it myself." I didn't wait for a response I hung up already making my decisions on what I had to do. My uncle thinks I didn't know why he was in my business but I knew.

Pouring some white Rum I drunk it straight hoping I would be able to get some sleep. I just wanted Sarai in my arms. I felt like a straight up bitch the way she stayed on my mind. Knowing someone had fucked with her was making shit ten times worse. Picking up the phone I used for her and mama I clicked the name wifey. She answered on the second ring so that told me even though it was late she wasn't asleep.

"Lucifer are you ok," she asked, surprise and concern in her voice? I watched as she tried to see me in the dark room. She looked adorable in one of the orange Armani shirts I left at the house. Her hair was tied up in a white scarf and her long legs were bare, causing my dick to swell and a chill to run through my body.

"Ma I'm cool. Honestly I missed you, I just needed to see your face." I didn't want to press her about the shit with Fabian because in the past I pushed too hard, to the point of being disrespectful every time some shit went down. Plus I wanted her to get back to a place where she would tell me when something was wrong. It was crazy as fuck how no matter how I tried to stay away from her I just couldn't. If I didn't fear what I would do to her she would be here with me now. Her and Mulan. I wouldn't be alone in the dark missing her. My mother did this, she created this monster and now I am a man who cannot even trust himself. "Damn you know that's not no night shirt B," I said just to get her to laugh, and she did. Her face blushed and her dimples popped out.

"It was just for tonight," she explained sheepishly. Shit she could wear whatever she wanted. I didn't give a fuck, she could really have whatever she wanted she just never asked. "You just calling because your boy is a snitching ass nigga." She was going in on Scar and I just sat there grinning. I was glad to see her little temper. "He needed to mind his business, I had it handled. I'm good and Mulan is good. He didn't bother me one fucking bit," she said with confidence, maybe too much.

"Who you trying to convince ma, me or you," I asked making her pause. She flipped over onto her stomach and propped the phone on the pillows. Dropping her head into her hands she looked my way. I turned on the TV so she could see my face. I was serious as fuck right now and I needed her to know that. "Come on shorty, if you was that fucking unbothered why you up at two in the morning."

A tear slid down her cheek and I felt my chest burn with rage. Scar didn't say this nigga hurt her but if he did that was his life. His whole family lives. I let him slide once and that was my fucking mistake, but it wouldn't happen again. She didn't say anything and I didn't push, just watched the one tear silently move from her chin onto her hand. She took a deep breath and I wondered if what she was going to say would be that bad. "Lynk I was up because of you. I want you here, I need you. I would do anything for you to just hold me for one more night. Please come home Lynk, please," she pleaded. Her tears came in a flood then, she buried her face in the pillow so I couldn't see her nose turn red and her eyes get all puffy. Damn I wanted the same thing but I just couldn't.

"Yo don't fucking cry. Come on, I'm here wit you right now ma. You know if I could be there I would, I just can't." She looked up at me with her tear stained eyes and broke my fucking heart. I wondered if I would hurt her like I did the others. I loved her like I never loved anyone else. When she was hurting so was I. That had to make shit different. Picturing the women's beaten and broken bodies in my mind, some dead, some wishing they were dead I knew I couldn't chance it.

"Will you ever be here again, will I ever see you again," she asked, her voice wobbly. I looked away, letting my hand rub my chin I couldn't answer her. I didn't know what to say.

"Come on all this crying shit not good for you. Pull the covers over your ass and let's go to sleep. You want me to tell you a story? You my little baby," I said laughing. I watched as she slid under the thick white comforter. Seeing her curl up to a pink pillow I smiled, she really took over a real niggas room and made that shit her own.

"I don't want a story, just don't hang up." She curled up putting the phone next to her face. I watched her watch me until she couldn't keep her eyes opened any longer. I didn't hang up just watched her sleep until the sun was shining and I could hear Mulan calling for Mama. I hung up as soon as she started to lift her head. I didn't want her to know how gone I was off her ass.

***

"What's she been up to," I asked Man as I leaned back in my California king bed? The doors to the upstairs veranda where open and the breeze caressed my face like a smooth bitches touch. I listened to all the drama from back home occasionally offering a grunt or an uh huh so Man knew I was still there. All I was really waiting on was the update I asked for on Sarai. I hadn't talked to her since the night I watched her sleep, the night she begged me to come home and since then I had been to Trinidad, L.A. and back to Trinidad.

"Man you shorty doing good, I be seeing her outside jogging early as fuck. That ass done got thick as fuck-"

"Her ass done got what nigga," I interrupted him before he could say another word. "Don't fucking ever look at her ass again." I was mad as fuck. I swear these young ones these days acted like they were getting high on the shit they were selling. "I will kill you, keep your eyes to your damn self." I did notice that her body was thicker last time we facetimed. Damn I needed to feel her.

"Sorry boss, didn't mean it like that," he apologized, fear in his voice. "Anyway she goes to college now, never misses a day. No niggas been at the house and all she do really is hang out with Scar and Tsunami bitches." Clearing my throat he rethought what he just said. "I mean their

A GHETTO LOVE STORY 3

girlfriends," he said fixing his mistake. "Oh some basketball player looking ass nigga tried to holler at her in the club the other night. I 'm not sure if she took his number or anything but I haven't seen him around after so I guess she didn't." That made my fist clench and sweat roll down my forehead. All I could see was red and I couldn't even hear man talking anymore. I threw the phone down on the bed and tried to get my anger under control. I knew it was time to leave, I just had one more thing to do.

I hurried and booked a flight and packed up my shit. I had gotten some tourist shit like t-shirts for Mulan and the boys. I put everything by the front door before driving to the church where my mother was buried. Jumping out I walked to her grave, it didn't bear her name. She didn't deserve that, there was just a cross engraved on the front of the tombstone. I sat there for a while watching the sun get low in the distance. "Mama I have decided not to come back here again so this will be our final goodbye. I'm not sorry for killing you, watching the life leave your eyes as I stabbed you over and over again was the only thing that allowed me to move on. See if I didn't kill you, you would have killed me. I had to find a way to survive. The last time was a close call, when they tried to kill me on the beach I cried for my mother until I looked up and saw you watching them. Your eyes transfixed and a smile on your face."

I knew in that moment that she had put the whole thing together. She was the reason people thought I was evil, and she would do anything to get rid of that evil inside of me. She had her son, a small child kidnapped in the middle of the night and then watched as his throat was sliced. "I will never forgive you," I said running my hand along the scar I wore my whole life. A reminder of who I was, what I was. "I will never forgive you not because you tried to have me killed. Not for all the baptisms and cruel words. But because you turned me into someone who is not fit to be a husband or a father, someone women could never trust. You turned me into the type of person who killed his own child, you turned me into you. And now that I have found the one, the one I love and want to be with I'm not good enough for her. I can't trust myself not to hurt her because of the psycho you created."

I still sat there in the soft dirt. Not caring about the time or anything around me. I had turned my phones off so that it was just me and my mother. Thinking about the losses I had suffered in my lifetime I went through them like a catalogue in my head, one by one. People who left me or people I helped leave. When I got to Sarai and Mulan's face I began to cry. I had never cried before I didn't think I knew how but I didn't stop it. I wanted to yell to the Heavens and let my mother know I just wanted her to love me. But I didn't I kept that to myself. She didn't deserve to know that.

Chapter 6 - Run into My Arms

Xanaya

Leaving the hospital I couldn't believe that my aunt had hurt Tamir. I should have whooped her ass and just took him home with me from jump but that bitch played dirty bringing the cops with her. She knew without them Tsunami would have killed her ass on sight. Walking through the parking garage I swore I heard footsteps behind me but every time I turned around no one was there. This shit was getting frustrating now. I knew someone was stalking me but I didn't know what to do about it. In the past five days someone has slashed my tires, left dead roses on my doorstep and creepy letters on my windshield after I left work. For the first time in my life I was truly scared and I didn't know what to do. I finally took Favour to Miss May's house because I was honestly scared to leave him home.

Clutching the Taser I carried in my purse a little tighter I began walking faster. The footsteps got closer and I started to run. My heart was beating so fast and loud I couldn't even hear if anyone was still behind me. I looked up just in time to see that I was running right into Tsunami. "Xanaya what the fuck is going on," he asked grabbing me by my arms so I didn't drop to the ground. I stood bent over trying to catch my breath. Straightening I looked around feeling stupid because no one was around. "Xa, did someone do something to you," he asked his eyes scanning the garage and one hand on his gun?

"No I'm sorry. I umm thought someone was chasing me. Lately I just feel like someone has been watching me and then I heard footsteps. It was stupid. I'm sure it's nothing." I shook my head and gave a slight laugh.

"I don't like this shit at all. You need to tell Scar what's up ma." I shook my head in a hell no motion. "You Mya fam and I can't let nothing happen to you. Just make sure you keep your eyes open and if anything hit my line. Let me walk you to your car." Once we got there I noticed a dead mouse next to the driver side door. I didn't really call attention to it because I didn't want Tsunami to call Scar hot headed ass.

"Thanks Tsu and I'm so sorry Tamir got hurt. You know if I could have kept him with me I would have and when I see my aunt again she is getting fucked up on sight."

"I know you would have Xa, that shit wasn't your fault. Her mama just evil and bitter, but she will get hers." He gave me a hug and watched as I climbed in my car. I wanted to bring up the way he was treating Mya but decided now was not the time. They always seemed to figure stuff out and what did I know I couldn't keep a good relationship for shit. Starting the Maxima I pulled out and just drove around for a while too creeped out to go home and not really knowing where else to go. I rode by Scars house a few times but couldn't bring myself to go knock on the door. It was getting late and I had to go home eventually. I was supposed to work early in the morning. I thought about the deposits that Scar put directly in my bank account these days instead of in letters. He was generous but I knew how he could be and I didn't want to get caught out there depending on a man who would someday turn on me.

Stopping at this Jamaican spot Livies I grabbed a Jerk chicken meal so I didn't have to cook. Shit cooking for one person was pitiful as fuck anyway. My phone lit up on the seat next to me and I answered before looking. "Xanaya, I need you," my mother's voice cried out into the other end of the phone. I pulled over so I could snatch it from the seat next to me and take her off of speaker. I hadn't spoken to my mother since the day I found out she was hiding the letters from Scar. She had tried to reach out to me here and there but I always sent her to voice mail. Hearing the panic in her voice was the only thing that kept me from hanging up. "Xa please come help me. I tried to stop her from hurting the baby I swear but she wouldn't listen. When I grabbed her she hit me with a pan and shoved me down the stairs. I have to get out of here before she comes back. Xa I can't move my legs," she shrieked in between her sobs.

I couldn't ignore her cries for help. She was a bitch but still my mother and she was hurt trying to save Tamir. "Mom I'm on the way. Try not to move." I made a u turn in the middle of Chili and headed back across town to my aunt's apartment. I screeched to a stop and rammed the gear into park. I ran up the stairs and when I opened the main doors to the apartment. I found my mother sprawled on the floor, her body was twisted like a deformed pretzel and blood was trickling from a cut next to her eye. I wondered how no one else had found her all this time.

"Momma are you ok," I cried running to her side? I dialed 911 and gave them the address as she tried to answer. I just put up my hand to hush her. "Don't speak, the ambulance is on the way. It will be here soon." I sat on the floor holding my mother's hand trying not to cry like a small child. Her hand brushed my belly and she gave me a slight smile. "Yea ma another one," I answered the question in her eyes. I didn't want to tell her it was Scar's baby. I felt overprotective of him even though we were fighting. He still had my heart.

"Ma'am please move so we can put her on the stretcher," the paramedics directed as they picked my mother up and strapped her down. Her legs were limp like two spaghetti noodles that just came out of boiling hot water. As they rushed my mother out I reassured her I would be right behind the ambulance. "She's going to Strong," the young guy yelled as he started to shut the doors. My aunt strolled through the door and never even looked at her sister and I knew she saw her out there being put in a fucking ambulance. She jogged up the stairs with an annoyed look on her face. I made sure to follow right behind, this bitch thought she was annoyed now. She had me fucked up if she thought she was going to keep getting away with this shit. When she saw me behind her she tried to run in her apartment and shut the door but I kicked that bitch in so hard it flew off the hinges and fell on her shaky ass.

"You crack head looking bitch," I yelled as I began stomping her with my feet. The blood was staining my pink Adidas and splattering my light blue jeans. "You fucked with my mother and my cousin. I'm so fucking tired of you." I took all my anger and frustrations out on her. I could still feel the heartbreak I felt the moment I saw Shelly and Scar, I put that rage into every hit. I kicked her in the ribs then picked up the closest weapon I could find, a mop with a wooden handle. Slamming it down on her back I couldn't stop hitting her. She laid there motionless like a dead dog and I didn't feel one once of sadness. I thought for a few minutes how I may end up in jail behind this shit but I guess it would have been worth it. Wiping the mop down with bleach I wiped everything I touched and left. I would burn my clothes and shoes once I made it home. She could rot in hell.

I had to go and change my clothes before I went to the hospital but I really didn't want to waste the time.

Remembering I had my gym clothes in the trunk I changed in the backseat of my car. Carefully wrapping up the bloody shit before putting it in my gym bag. My heart wouldn't let me go home first because I needed to make sure my mom was ok. Parking I felt like all I been doing the past year was come to hospitals and I was tired of that shit. I needed to have this baby at home or something because I swear the Roc had some evil shit going on and we always ended up right back here. Making my way to the information desk I swear it was the same lady from last time I was here.

"Hello I'm looking for my mother, her name is Sandrine Davis and she was brought in by ambulance." I tried to smile as she began typing away on her computer but I knew it fell short.

"Ma'am she was rushed into surgery. I can show you to the waiting room for emergency patients and a doctor will come alert you on her condition when they can." She gave me a look of pity as she led me down the hallway I was beginning to know all too well. I sunk down in the hard plastic chair and closed my eyes. After what seemed like hours I decided to call Jason, my brother's dad. I didn't know what these doctors were going to say and I needed someone to go through this shit with me. He always treated me well even after him and my mom broke up. He was the closest thing I had to a father.

"Hey Xanaya, how have you been? You should call more often and come visit your brother really misses you," Jason said as he answered me on the second ring. I couldn't help but to cry, I tried to speak but no words came out. "Xanaya is everything ok," he asked in a serious tone.

"No, it's my mom she was injured. Well thrown down some stairs and she's still in surgery. I just wondered if you could come here because I don't know what to do. I just need somebody to help me and my aunt is the one who did this to her. I didn't know who else to call. We are at Strong Hospital if you could please come." I was rocking back and forth because I was so distressed.

"Xa calm down, I'm already on my way. We will be there in less than an hour just hold on baby girl. Is there anyone you can call to come and be with you sooner?" I thought about it and came up with a blank because Mya was in a room upstairs and me and Scar were fucked up like always. Damn I didn't even have any friends. I thought about Sarai and decided to call her. She was closer with Mya but I knew she would come.

"Yes I do, I will call her right now," I said reassuring him. I sent Sarai a text and she told me she would be here in ten minutes. I sat staring at my hands for a while just trying to calm down. I knew all this stress wasn't good for my baby. Shit I was almost four months pregnant and barely showing. I couldn't tell you when I slowed down enough to eat or sleep between being at the hospital, my job or running behind Favour.

Sarai came running down the hallway. I could tell she really rushed out because she had on a pair of brown Uggs, blue sweat pants and a pink hoodie. Her hair was still in her bonnet and she had on no earrings or make up. "Xa it's going to be ok," she said flinging herself onto the chair next to me and wrapping her arms around me. I relaxed a little grateful for some support. "Did you eat," she asked her eyebrow raised? I nodded my head no and she frowned. "Naw you playing, you better go feed this baby. Shit Mya got Favour but this one is gonna be my God baby and you better treat her right."

"Shit I hope it is a girl Favour bad as fuck. I will eat something if you stop staring at me like that. Bossy ass," I said talking shit.

"Yea I'm bossy because I love you ass," she shot back.

Standing up I noticed a doctor wander from the back looking at his chart. "Family of Sandrine Davis," he said looking around. I jumped up just as Jason, my brother and a coco brown lady with a fur coat walked in. Khayson ran up to me and flung his arms around me. I kissed his forehead smoothing the curly hair back. He had gotten so big since I last saw him.

"We are her family Jason said as we all walked forward. His female friend hung back respectfully. I wasn't even mad he moved on, shit she was cute and seemed to have a better attitude than my mom.

"Ok, she has made it out of the surgery fine but her spine is damaged and I'm afraid she will never walk again. She won't be awake for several hours so all you can do is wait now while she is in recovery. She should be able to have visitors by tomorrow and we will have a full update." He turned and walked away at ease like he didn't just shatter my world. My mom wouldn't take being paralyzed well. She was always on the go, active and outgoing. This would kill her.

Not wanting my little brother to know how terrible things really were I talked to him a little before I got ready to go. Walking up to Jason I welcomed his hug. "Jason thank you for coming. I'm sure you didn't want to. I know it's a burden making that drive. Mom always told me how you hated it that's why we couldn't see Khayson, but you came when it really counted."

"Sweetie there is a lot about your mother that you don't know. I won't go into to many details because she is up there fighting for her life but please know I would have never kept your brother from you. Your mother told me not to bring him because she didn't want to be bothered. When I heard she put you out for being pregnant I told her we would take you. Felicia, that's my wife had no problem with you and the baby coming to live with us. But your mother told me to go to hell and I didn't have a number for you at the time. Now that's enough of that because at the end of the day she is suffering and she's still your mother. Just know you have a family here if you need one. Now you go get some rest, you look exhausted."

"Thank You," I whispered. I meant it too, not just for being there but for trying to always be there and for taking care of my brother. I had no idea my mother was doing all this bullshit. Standing in the main hallway I took out my phone and my hand shook. All I wanted to do was call him, just have him come and be with me because I needed his presence, his love. Chickening out I put the phone away and looked at Sarai. "Let's go see Mya," I asked, my eyes pleading with her to say sure.

"Come on, she will be happy for some company I'm sure." We made it upstairs in no time and Mya was sitting up cussing at an episode of Jeopardy.

"Damn what Jeopardy do to yo lil ass," I said as I carefully got on the bed beside her. I tried to sound cheerful but my cousin knew me to my core. She looked me up and down and put her arms around me. I didn't want to explain everything that had happened that day but I couldn't stop the tears. I curled up to my cousin and felt Sarai throw a blanket over me. She pulled up a chair next to the bed and put her next to mine. We all stayed like that until the morning. I woke up feeling squished as hell but happy no punk ass nurses came in here fucking with us.

"You ready to go see your mom," Sarai asked as she came from the bathroom.

"Yea let's go," I said going to brush my teeth and wash my face. I felt a little better than the night before. Mya and Sarai were my strength and I appreciated that. I came out to Mya putting on some leggings and a green hoodie. She slid her feet into some matching furry green slides and walked to the door. "Boo where you think you going all shot the fuck up and shit," I asked?

"Xa you not the boss of me, you see my injured ass holding this door now let's go," she said walking out. I followed letting Mya be there for me. Once we found the room I noticed Jason was there but his wife and my brother were not. He sat in the corner with his hands in his head and I knew it wasn't good. My mother was awake but her eyes looked dead. Maybe she was high off the meds.

"Good Morning Mom," I said as I walked closer to her and went to kiss her cheek. She turned her head away from me and faced the wall. "Ma talk to me what's wrong," I pleaded?

"Why are you here Xanaya," she asked with an attitude? "Don't you need to go run to your drug dealing ass boyfriend and check on him, oh wait I guess he would be baby father now huh." She gave a bitter laugh as she looked me up and down with her cold and distant eyes. "Xanaya to answer your question you want to know what's wrong? I will never fucking walk again, you're here and oh yea you decided to call this bitch ass nigga to come up here for what I don't even know." I was trying not to cuss my mama out since she just found out she would never walk again. I was shocked because I wasn't expecting that. I guess no one could this shit just happened. I wanted to tell her how I fucked her sister up for what she did to her but I couldn't with a room full of people.

"Sandrine you don't have to talk to her like that what fuck. You asked like she begged you to conceive her. Yea you going through something but you're the fucking mom." Jason stood up looking at her in disgust as he spoke. If my mom wasn't already in a hospital he might have made it happen by the anger I could feel radiating off of him.

"Hey Jason you want to know something, fuck you. That's why Xanaya is your daughter I just never told you because you're a bitch. So fuck you and her and ya'll can both get the fuck out." My mom smirked at us both but not for long. Jason grabbed her by her throat and began choking the life out of her.

"Bitch when you told me you had a kid I asked you more than once was she mine and you said no. That's why I stopped fucking wit your sneaky ass in the first place. You made me miss out on my daughter's whole life. You didn't give a fuck about me or her and clearly not my son. Had I known she was mine I would have taken her from your raggedy ass a long time ago! You hide behind that professional job and act like you aint still just a ratchet hoe from the projects." He gripped her neck a while longer as her brown face turned purple.

"Don't," I cried out wanting it all to just stop. He dropped my mother like she was burning him. He walked over to me and held me in his arms. All these years I had a dad, shit a good one but he didn't know and I didn't know. My mother was pure evil just like her sister. That shit must have run in their family. I prayed me and my cousin didn't inherit any of that shit. "I need to go," I said as I pushed away from him. It was all just too much for me to handle. I needed Scar, only he could make me feel better.

"I understand, please once you get your emotions together call me. If you need me call me. I'm your dad and I want to make up for everything. I should have just had you tested this is my fault." Jason said as I ran out of the room.

Scar

My phone buzzed across the table. Looking at it I hoped it was Xanaya. Letting out a sigh as I saw Shelly's name flash across the screen and I hit reject. I swear ever since she found out I had a kid with Xanaya she had become the biggest pain in the ass. I never used to spend time with her kid, just give her money and keep it moving. Now she wanted a family complete with me playing the daddy and husband. I wasn't being a fuckboy, when she told me she was pregnant I told her two things. One it wasn't mine and two that she should get rid of it because I had a girl at home. She didn't and I took care of the little boy even though he aint have shit for me and I made it clear I didn't want a baby with her. We looked like complete strangers. Seeing the phone ring again I picked up, "man what Shelly, I'm over here trying to get fucked and sucked. I just gave yo ass money yesterday so what the fuck you want now," I snapped into the phone.

Even though the sun just came from behind the clouds I needed a fucking drink. I had to meet up with some niggas from the west at three who wanted to cop a few bricks. Then I was dropping by my lawyer's office to see when I was going to be able to see my fucking son. Hanging up on her whining ass after I saw she aint want nothing but the same shit, I stumbled my way to the bar that was in the living room. I opened a new bottle of Patron and threw it in a cup. I splashed some orange juice in there just to make it feel like breakfast. I could hear movement from my basement and I made a mental note to visit my hostage before I hit the road.

"Scar you coming back to bed," asked the naked girl who walked out of my bedroom. Shit I didn't even remember bringing that bitch back to my crib the night before. Another girl came out after her except she was fully clothed and had an ugly ass green purse she was holding onto like I was about to steal her shit. She needed to return her Nanas hand bag.

"Thanks ladies for coming to visit. Just top me off right fast and you both can bounce," I instructed dropping my baller shorts and settling myself on the couch. The red head naked girl immediately dropped to her knees and took my dick in her mouth. The other girl stood there looking like the cleaning lady who walked in on us. Straight up scared and shook, shit I must have really been fucked up to bring her home. I crooked my finger and motioned for her to come on. Finally she walked my way and fell to her knees. She wasn't very graceful because she almost knocked over the other shorty and ended up falling into my lap. Frowning up my face I shoved her so she fell to the floor. "Bitch do better what the fuck."

She peeled off her purple crop top and stepped out of her Old Navy flip flops and blue jeans. She had no bra or panties on and I hope she aint leave that shit somewhere in my house. The red head started tugging on the other girls nipples and rubbing her dry ass pussy. Miss stuck up let her guard down and took my whole dick in her mouth. As soon as I felt the back of her throat the freak session was interrupted when my front door flew open. Jumping up I knocked both those bitches down in the process of grabbing my nine from behind the couch cushion. "Ya'll bitches get out," Xanaya yelled kicking the red head in her side like she was a stray dog. I pulled up my shorts and watched my company scramble around grabbing clothes and shit.

I didn't stop her I just sat back and watched as Xanaya

terrorized the two females. The red head tried to swing on her while her back was turned but I grabbed her wrist in mid swing. I almost broke her shit I snatched it so hard. "Nah bitch that's wifey, now get the fuck out." Xa kept right on not even paying me any attention. She looked so fucking pretty to me even when she was creating chaos. Even through her Pink North Face jacket I could see her round belly, her face was turning red from all the yelling and cursing she was doing and her hazel eyes were getting darker the angrier she got.

As soon as the door closed behind the panicked girls Xa locked it and made her way to my bedroom. I wanted to ask her how the fuck she even knew where I lived, not to mention how she got in. She never stopped to take off her coat just started stripping the sheets and blankets off the bed and flinging them in the hallway. When she finished she took off her jackets and boots and tossed a pink keychain on the bedside table. Well at least I knew where she got the key, it was the one Love had in case of an emergency. I wasn't even mad shit, Xa was the only one who could bust in my shit.

She stood there staring at me for a few minutes with tears swimming in her eyes. I was waiting on her to start talking shit but it didn't happen. She stomped her way into the hallway and flung open the closet. She walked back in with sheets and a new comforter. After making the bed she was huffing and puffing and looked exhausted. I noticed the bags under her eyes and I wondered was she ok. Suddenly she looked green and began gagging. I pointed to the bathroom and she ran in slamming the door in my face. I was about to see if she was good but fuck it. I could hear shorty throwing up her fucking guts and I felt bad for her. I guess my baby was giving her hell. Opening the bathroom door she brushed past me like I wasn't even there. She been in my crib like an hour and hadn't said a fucking word to me. She undressed neatly folding her jeans and shirt on the top of my dresser. Seeing her purple lace thong and bra made my dick rock up.

She threw on my white tee and threw herself in my bed. Grabbing a pillow she held on to it and started to cry. I didn't know what to do so I slid in the bed next to her. Throwing the pillow to the other side of the bed I pulled her to me. Her hot tears soaked my shirt as she burrowed into me. Running my hands over her back I was just happy that she was in my presence. She needed me and nothing else had to be said. "Babe what's up," I asked running my hand up and down her back.

"My mom is paralyzed and she lied about my dad, he was alive and around but she lied to us both. I think I killed my aunt yesterday and I think someone is stalking me. It's all too much Sciony and I can't keep doing this. I need someone, I need you." She stopped talking and clung on to me. Damn my shorty been going through mad shit and I been over here just living life. When she said someone was stalking her my head started to pound because I still hadn't caught M and now this nigga was coming for my girl. *Fuck.*

"Shorty you got me always ma, I aint going anywhere. Just stop shutting a nigga out, let me yo man like I'm supposed to." She nodded her head and started kissing me. I thought about the bitch sucking my dick right before she got there and I stopped her. It would have been easy to just fuck her right now but I wasn't that low. "Come on babe get some rest. I got to go to a business meeting soon but I want you to stay here. You good here ma and I won't be gone long. Just stay out the basement my dogs don't know yo ass and I don't want them eating your little ass." She rolled her eyes and held on to me tighter.

"Just stay with me a little longer," she said. I didn't hesitate to give my girl whatever the fuck she wanted.

Kissing the top of her head I settled back in the bed and watched as she fell asleep. Eventually I crept out of the bed and threw on some black Levi jeans, a brown hoodie and wheat Timbs. I drove my black BMW out to Scottsville where we had some chill house we used for business. Tsunami was there before me looking like he had the fucking world on his shoulders.

"What up my nigga," I said and we gave each other dap. I knew I had to tell him about Chania because M was getting to close to Xa and getting that bitch to talk was now a fucking priority. Look I need to talk to you on some real shit. I know you figured out Chania had some shit to do with Mya getting shot." He nodded his head looking out in the distance like nothing even mattered to him. "Nigga you listening, she was working with some cat named M and they was trying to kill Xanaya so she could get with me. It was never about Mya or you." His head snapped up and he was giving me a death stare.

"How the fuck you know," he asked suspicion in his voice.

"Because Chania ass tied up in my basement son, I was waiting for you to get yo girl together and make sure your lil one was good. You can do what you want with her ass but she has to tell me who M is because someone is stalking Xa." I could tell he was pissed off. He held it good though. His face stayed the same, blank but his body had tightened up like he wanted to fight my ass.

"This some fuck shit son, you just waited all this fucking time to say something. I'm going to handle Chania ass as soon as we done with Marco." He leaned back against the wooden post on the porch and rolled a blunt. I knew his head was fucked up because this nigga didn't smoke like I did.

Marco came and we went over our numbers and

expectations from him. The meeting was wrapping up when my phone rang, seeing Xa calling I sent her to voicemail. She knew when I was handling business that I didn't take calls. She called back two more times and I gave Tsunami a look. I had to answer with M crazy ass still on the loose. "Yo," I answered not sure what was going on.

"You need to get home and see about your basement house guest," she said laughing before she hung up.

Walking back to Marco and Tsunami I gave that nigga a look. "Aight Marco we going to have to get up out of here so just hit up my nigga Man in a few days and he will have that shit ready for you." We both moved fast as a bitch and hopped in our whips. "Your crib," he asked?

"Yea, Xanaya went snooping in the basement."

I got home in less than ten minutes because I didn't know what the fuck Xa crazy ass had going on. Next thing she will be accusing me of fucking with Chania ass. Me and Tsunami got there at the same time. Walking in the house it was dead ass quiet. I went straight to the basement but stopped short when I saw all the blood. Grabbing Xanaya by her arm I shook her. "What the fuck is wrong wit you yo," she looked at me with a mug on her face as the knife fell to the ground. I heard growling only to see my dog standing in front of her ready to go on my ass. "Naya go home," I yelled and she barked once before going to her cage.

"Nigga you named a dog after me, really Scar," she fussed not addressing the fact that Chania sat in the chair with her throat slashed open.

"Xanaya why you do this bullshit man, this was for me to do. Now we don't even fucking know who she was working with." Tsunami said screaming on her ass. I was about to check that nigga when Xa moved around me and got in his face. Well tried to since he was taller than her.

She stood on her tiptoes and rolled her neck. "Nigga watch who you talking too before you are next. I know you in your feelings because that's your sister but don't take that shit out on me. I swear ya'll nigga's always act like woman are stupid. Of course I know who is after me." She began petting the dogs like she didn't just drop a bomb. We stood there staring at her. "Oh M is Malik."

Chapter 7 - Masks Off

Sarai

My days were so busy since I started school I didn't know if I was coming or going. Grabbing Mulan from the daycare I scrambled to carry her and all my books as we walked to the car. I let her go to the daycare center at my college so she would be close. On days I got lazy I took her to Tsunami's grandmother. She was the only one who helped so I could get a break these days unless Mya or Xanaya got my baby. Somedays having no family made shit really hard but I was grateful for who I had. After what seemed like forever since we had to drive slowly in the snow I made it home. There was a strange car parked in front of my house that made me worried. I didn't get visitors I didn't know and I wondered for a moment if Fabian had come to fuck with me. As I got closer I noticed the car was a Taxi. Who even takes a Taxi these days with Uber and Lyft.

I parked and Mama Carrie climbed out of the back. "Mama why didn't you just go inside, I'm sure you have a key?" I jumped out to help her with his bags and give her a hug.

"Honey I would have called you if it was taking too long. I didn't want to wait in the house and scare you or you walk in and scare me. I'm old I can't be having no heart attacks." She laughed and gave me another hug.

I was genuinely happy to have her here because it was lonely sometimes plus me and Mulan loved her. "Come inside its so cold out here." I got Mulan out of the car and unlocked the door. "What are you doing here especially in all this cold weather?" I asked as I took her coat.

"I was lonely in Florida all by myself. Plus I missed my grand baby. I was hoping I would have another one on the way but that doesn't look like the case. Yet," she said as she looked me up and down. I shrugged and felt myself turning red. Hell I was wishing for a baby with her grandson too but it was hard to get pregnant by someone who wasn't here.

"Well come in we are happy you're here. I'm not always home because I'm in school now. But you're welcome to stay as long as you want." I made my way to the kitchen and started taking out some chicken for dinner. I hadn't really been cooking since it was just me and Mulan but I wanted Mama Carrie to be good. Pulling out some French green beans and rice I started to cook. I smiled as Mulan brought out every toy she could carry and set them on the couch next to Mama. She was so excited. Clapping her tiny hands and running on her fat legs. I finished cooking and set the table so we could eat. After dinner I put Mulan to bed and me and Mama Carrie set down on the couches sipping hot cocoa. I told her about everything that has been going on from Mya getting shot to Xanaya's mother being paralyzed. It was so easy to talk to her and I felt like a weight had been lifted off my shoulders when I was done. She listened a lot not really commenting until I told her about the Fabian thing.

"Don't worry about that little boy Fabian, I know Lucifer will never let anyone hurt you or Mulan. He would die first so please don't allow that idiot boy get to you." I must have given her a doubtful look because she got up and made her way to her purse. Walking back she held a small long box with a little card attached to it. Mama sat down next to me and grabbed my hands. "Sarai do you think that Lucifer doesn't love you," she asked looking in my eyes. I shrugged my shoulders like a child not really knowing how to answer. I didn't think he loved me most of the time but some days I was convinced he did. It was so damn confusing, hell he was so confusing.

"Sarai do you love him," her eyes were so serious. I was kind of nervous were this was going.

"Yes I do love him. I have never loved anyone the way I do him. I think about him every day even if we don't talk. He's my strength, my comfort and my best friend. Before we messed everything up, before I messed everything up I mean and drove him away we talked every day. I miss that more than anything. He would make me laugh no matter what was going on. I miss him," I finished hanging my head down as I felt the sadness wash over me.

"Sarai he loves you, he doesn't own the words to say it or understand the way to show it but I know he does. You didn't do anything to run him away except be the only women he has ever cared about aside from me. Lynk is scare. He doesn't want to hurt you." I looked at her with my eyes bucked. Hell he was doing a good job of hurting me now. My heart was sitting in my chest being held together with invisible bandages. "Yes he has hurt your heart but he is worried about hurting you. There is a lot you don't know about Lynk. He is damaged and he has acted out on those feelings many times in the past. How much do you love him Sarai? Can you handle all he is facing, his demons that haunt him, his anger?"

"Mama I'm not in the dark to Lynks challenges. I know about his brush with death as a child. I know about his mother trying to get the devil out of him. I have accepted him for who he is because that's what real love is all about. Plus everything he has been through shaped him to be the man I respect and want by my side." She leaned back and stared into space for a few minutes. I thought she may have been praying. She looked like she was carrying the burden now. "Mama are you ok," I asked lightly touching her arm.

"Yes I have been going back and forth with this decision for a while but the time has come and I have to do this. When I found the card and the gift I knew. Then Lynk updated his will and I was sure. He had never had a thought in his head for anyone else all these years. I watched him sleep with women and abandon them like trash. Nothing mattered except money and the streets until he met you. He thought my feelings would be hurt when he added you to his will but I told him I planned to be long dead before he was. Plus I knew the day I met you that you were the one."

"Anyway I'm all over the place. Call it an old persons mind if you will. Sarai you don't know the whole story of Lucifer but I'm going to tell you." I sat and listened for an hour as Mama Carrie talked about all Lynk had been through and some of the things he had done. I will admit a part of me felt fear hearing some of the stuff but I knew he wouldn't hurt me the way he did others. When she finished I had tears streaming down my face. I wasn't crying for me, I was crying for the man I loved. For all the pain he had experienced and all the people who had betrayed him starting with his own mother. "The last thing I had to do was give this to you." She handed me the box with the small card attached. "Lynk left this with me just in case something happened to him. He wanted you to have this after he was gone but you should have it now, I am going to bed sweetie. Have a good night."

She stood up and hugged me before going upstairs to the guest room she would be staying in. I sat in the same spot for a while holding the long box turning it over again and again. Finally I opened it. Inside was a delicate platinum necklace with a praying angel pendant. Diamonds surrounded her hands. Turning it over I read the simple inscription, *love you always, Lynk*. I put it on right away, it made me feel closer to Lynk even though I had no idea where he was. My hands shook as I opened the card. It was white with nothing on the outside. On the inside I recognized his bold writing.

Sarai if you're reading this I'm gone, dead, you know how this street shit goes. I never had the courage to tell you what I have done but just know I earned the name Lucifer in this lifetime. I couldn't allow you to become one of my casualties so I ran away. I wish it could have been different because God knows I wanted you, will want you until the day I take my last breath. Sarai the only way I can show you I love you is this way. I left everything I have to you and Mulan. I couldn't love you in life so I will love you in death. Love always Lucifer.

I was shocked, I didn't want his money I wanted him. I needed to be near him. I didn't care where he was or what he had done. I went to bed that night with a lot on my mind. I tossed and turned until the alarm went off early and my routine began. I was running a little late so I skipped my work out. Trying to be quiet I woke Mulan up and had to chase her around to get dressed. "Mulan, not today honey mommy has to go," I said as low as I could.

"Where exactly is Mulan going," Mama Carrie asked standing at her bedroom doorway.

"Daycare Mama, I have class today. I'm sorry we woke you up I was trying to keep her quiet but she has no off button." I snagged Mulan and flung her over my shoulder which made her laugh.

"No I don't want her in a daycare you will leave her here with me. This is why you should move to Florida. My baby needs her Mama not strangers." She grabbed Mulan from me and waved me off to go get dressed. I hoped she didn't get overwhelmed but I was happy my baby would be home getting one on one care from someone who loved her. I ran to throw on my clothes so I could hurry out to Brockport.

*****

Mama had been with me for a few weeks and I loved it. I came home to dinner and a clean house. Xanaya and Mya wanted to steal her and called me spoiled. I finished the first quarter with straight A's and was ready for my upcoming winter break. I heard Mama say that Lynk was in Florida now so I made a decision to go and find him. But before I left I had some unfinished business.

Checking the time I was happy to see it was six pm. I knew right where they would be. Grabbing a knife from the kitchen I stuck it in my purse. I pulled on a pair of black Timbs and checked on Mama. She was rocking Mulan and watching some Judge show. "Mama, I'm running out for a few minutes. Is there anything you need from the store?"

"No baby I am all set," she said smiling her wide smile.

I drove to the church where I spent many hear-broken days and evenings. I could still see the lights on and my aunts car was parked in he assigned spot. Tonight was spaghetti dinner night and they never missed. I took a few minutes to look in the mirror of the car and pep tak myself. But as soon as the reflection caught the necklace Lynk gave me I felt all the strength I needed. He loved me, even if not one other person did and that was ok.

Opening the side door I climbed down the stairs to the huge basement that was turned into a coffee time meet and greet area. There were tables everywhere and it looked like everyone from the church had come out to eat spaghetti.

I stood observing them for a little while. They sat there like the king and queen of Christianity. My aunt remained bossy as she used her hands to tell people what to do. "Hello Aunt and Uncle," I said as I walked in front of them. I rolled my eyes and made sure to let them see my scowl. I wanted to run away because I knew what their hurtful words could do to my soul but I was stronger now.

"I just wanted to say to you that what you did was wrong. Why take in a child, an innocent child if you were only going to mistreat her? I don't really need a response," I said as I held up my hand to stop the protest my uncle already had ready on his thick disgusting lips. I could hear the other church members around us gasp in shock. "You spent years blaming me for my mother and sisters murders. You made me feel worse that I already felt. You had me feeling guilty for living when they died. I was a CHILD, IT WAS NOT MY FAULT!!" Screaming I felt all the anger and rage I had carried around with me come tumbling out. I couldn't control myself. The tears I cried felt cleansing. Reaching out and slapping my aunt across her smug face I was satisfied at the loud crack I heard. "That was for everything, and to leave you with a reminder. You should treat people better. I was more than a charity case you could brag about taking in to your fake ass church friends."

I turned and walked away before anyone could say another word. Speeding home I stopped at the seven eleven and picked up a red bull. I had a lot to do tonight. After driving I was happy to see home, even if it was only temporary. Grabbing my laptop I smiled imaging being close to Lynk again. If he was scared of loving me I would just have to make him unscared. Scrolling tickets I found some good ones and went to tell Mama we were going back to Miami. I was going to get my man.

Lynk

Sitting at the outdoor table looking at my Uncle as he sipped his tea I knew picking a public place was a good idea so he could keep his brains on the inside of his body. "Lynk are you listening to what I'm telling you? All this is going to be yours. I'm handing my entire empire to you." He looked at me with an expression of pride and joy. All I felt inside was disgust for this half a fucking man sitting in front of me.

"Yo Unc or should I say Pops don't sit here and play games with me. You are giving me your empire because I fucking deserve it. When I sat watching my mother bleed to death she let that secret slip. The one where she fucked her husband's brother and had me," I made sure my voice dripped with venom so he knew how serious I was about the shit I was saying. You knew I was your son, you knew my mother tried to have me killed. I remember wishing my father would save me and wondering why he never came for me. I killed the wrong man, your brother paid for your sins. So Pastor Hughes what you're going to do is step down now, I'm now running all of this and you. Well you can retire peacefully or join your brother in his resting spot."

He sat there speechless. His mouth was slack and eyes watering with fake ass tears. I threw a hundred dollar bill on the table and jogged to my whip. Nobody told his punk ass to come to Miami looking for me anyway. He should have kept living his lie and left me the fuck alone.

*****

I tried to focus on Michelle's warm mouth as she worked double time to get me to bust all over her face. She loved the nasty shit. All I wanted to do was forget about the early morning meeting with my fake ass uncle. But honestly being back in the states had my soul more disturbed than ever before and it seemed like I couldn't release any of this stress that was on me. Three days here and all I had done was think about Mulan and Sarai, those were the only thoughts that gave me comfort. They were the same thoughts that brought me stress. I craved Sarai like a drug and I wasn't handling being without her well. Feeling teeth lightly scrape my dick I yanked her head up. "What the fuck is wrong wit you," I demanded holding her by her hair like she was a rag doll.

"Sorry," she slowly said but I could see the banked rage in her eyes. I knew she wanted to say something else or try me. Just her thoughts pissed me off and I felt my fist tightening in her hair. Why the fuck did I ever bring this bitch to my house. I never brought hoes here and all she was doing was frustrating me off more than I already was.

The rage she was holding bubbled over and her thoughts poured out and became words. "Stop abusing me because of her. If she doesn't want you because of who you are and what you have done, than accept it and move the fuck on. I have been here sucking and fucking you despite the monster that you are. Even knowing what I know I never turned my fucking back on you and you want to treat me like shit." She stopped and took a deep breath. I still had a grip on her but it was like her anger was making her immune to that shit.

"Lucifer you are a truly the devil, you walk around here with this entitled fucking attitude because what? You sexy, you got money? Or is it because you got a big ass dick? It doesn't change your black heart, your tainted soul if you even have one. You are nothing more than a murderer and I don't want your ass anymore." She crossed her arms over her breasts with an attitude and her eyes were sparking with her hurt and rage. I was counting to a hundred over and over again in my mind trying to keep calm. I could see she was going to do some dumb shit before she even did it. I told myself like a fucking mantra in my mind to let her go and walk away. I just couldn't loosen my grip.

Just like I envisioned she was on some bullshit, her hand slowly crept to the lamp next to her and grabbed it by the base. She snatched it and swung it at my head knocking the shit outta me. Her eyes grew wide with fear as I stood there with my hands still in her hair. I wouldn't be surprised if her scalp was bleeding that's how hard I was holding on. At the speed of light I had her against the wall, my fingers digging into her neck. Her legs dangled as I held her up and in that moment I no longer saw Michelle. Instead I saw Misa, her flawless skin, her lying ass mouth even after I caught her fucking my Uncle and her frightened eyes. I saw the way her hands went to her stomach as I choked the life out of her. She was trying to protect our baby, if only I had known.

I stopped choking Michelle and tried to just let her make it. "Yea I know you love that shit. Was that how you killed your woman and unborn child? Did it make you smile? You fucking murderer. I hate you Lynk more than you will ever know," she said her voice raspy from her throat being closed off for so long. What the fuck did she know about Misa and my unborn? All the blood rushed to my head and I couldn't think. I began banging her head against the wall. I wanted to kill her in that moment she was just like the rest of them. This was why I hated women.

"Lynk stop," I heard Sarai's voice call out to me through the fog I was in. Damn I was really fucked up hearing her like she was here. I needed help because on the real a nigga felt like he was going crazy. "LYNK," she yelled only this time her hand was on my arm. I dropped Michelle and spun around. She was there in front of me her face filled with fear, shock and something else I couldn't figure out. I was pretty sure it was disgust since she just heard that I had killed my girl and kid. I didn't mean to do it. I lost my temper and she fell. She hit her head and never woke up. I didn't even know she was pregnant. I would have been able to walk away had I known. At least that's what I told myself every day.

"You shouldn't be here," I mumbled trying not to look at her. I didn't want to feel the pain I knew I would when she rejected me. "Now you know the person you have been loving was not worth your heart.

"Lynk I love you, I already knew what happened. I don't care. I want you, please don't leave me." I looked at her then and noticed the necklace I had made for her. My grandmother had put her nose in my business. I wasn't sure how I felt, I knew she loved me and wanted the best for me. But she didn't understand that I'm broken. I kill men, women anyone who gets in my way or on my nerves and I never feel a thing. No remorse, not sadness. I was a real life monster.

"I will always leave you Sarai, look at what I've done. Look," I shouted pointing to Michelle who was on the ground half conscious. What if that was Sarai? What if I did that to her? I couldn't live with myself. She still stood there in front of me with love in her eyes. "Sarai I'm sorry but I can never truly love a woman. I hate women for all they have done to me and if I try to be with you I will lose my temper one day and then what? You could end up dead and then I couldn't live with myself. I can't do this, please just go." I watched as she walked slowly out of the room heartbroken once again because of me.

"Good stupid bitch, if he could love it would be me. And stay away or next time I will make sure your home for the fire," Michelle said through her swollen ass lips. Sarai lunged for her hitting her in her face. I grabbed her hard and pulled her out of the room. The only thing that saved Michelle's life at that moment was the fact that I got lost in Sarai. She clung onto me angry sobs leaving her mouth.

"She's the reason I was broken. If I would have been stronger you wouldn't have left me. I want her dead. It's not fair." She cried so hard she had to run in the bathroom and throw up. She thought I left her because she went through something. Damn. I paced the hallway running my hands over my three sixty waves trying to think. My mind was telling me to kill Michelle but my heart said not to. If I could let her walk away maybe I had a chance with Sarai. Maybe I could control my temper and maybe I wouldn't have to lose the woman I loved.

I stepped in the room to see Michelle huddled in a ball. Fear was all over her face. She knew what it meant to cross me and she knew what was next. "You have ten seconds to get the fuck out of here. If you ever come near Sarai again you won't have another chance. For the record this isn't about you, I don't give a fuck about yo ass and killing you wouldn't even phase me. This is about her, the woman I do love. No GO," I demanded. She moved faster than I ever saw her move. A moment later I heard my front door slam and saw her screech out of my driveway.

"You let her go," Sarai yelled. She walked over and slapped me in my face so my head snapped back. Her face became wide with fear once she realized what she did. I stood still waiting for the uncontrollable rage to come but it didn't. I wanted to punish her by fucking her little ass I didn't want to hurt her. Walking up on her I grabbed her arms gently and leaned in to kiss her lips. I felt her small hands frame my face and I forgot everything else.

I knew I had to explain to her because she was my world and I didn't want her walking around feeling like I dubbed her ass over Michelle. "Listen ma, I let her go because that shit can't be me anymore. You want me to be wit you and shit then I have to know I can control myself. If I killed Michelle than I was still that nigga who would have hurt you, I don't want to be that nigga." She wrapped her arms around me and laid her head on my chest. I felt my heart racing and that little voice inside told me to run. But my heart and my soul kept me right there.

Chapter 8 - Standing On My Own

Kahmya

"Thanks," I mumbled sadly to Xanaya as she pulled up to my house and hit the locks on her car.

"Kahmya, do you want me to come inside with you? I can stay the night, you shouldn't be alone. Or you can just grab some clothes and come to my house. Scar ass crazy but you know you lil cuz to him he won't care and if he do he can go drop himself off at a fire station or some shit where someone might care." I shook my head and laughed a little. I couldn't believe it when she said her and Scar was really going to be together. She was rude as fuck so I was praying for Scar.

"Nope I got to live alone since Tsunami ass just got rid of me so let me just get used to it from now. Anyway in a few days Tamir will be home with his mama where he belongs so I need to get my house together."

"Ok, well let me carry your stuff in. Don't worry about the house you know me and Sarai cleaned the shit out of it already."

"Xa what the fuck happened to Chania? I haven't seen her and it doesn't seem like you guys have been hanging out with her or anything," I asked with worry in my voice. Chania was like my sister and I couldn't see her not being by my side the whole time I was down and out. Maybe she was sick again. Xanaya gave me a strange look as she came in and sat on the edge of the couch. "What Xa, just tell me. I have known you my whole life and I know that look."

"I don't really know how to say this. You have already been through so much but I will just say this shit. Chania wasn't really the friend you thought she was. You being shot was her fault." I had to sit down and fast because I thought I was going to faint. Why would Chania want me dead? I had always been good to her and I thought she loved me. Was no one able to truly love me? I couldn't help the tears, maybe it was because of all I been through or the baby I was carrying but I felt devastated. "Come on My don't get so upset. It wasn't about you. It was about me, well Scar. She was in love with him to the point it drove her crazy. She was working with Malik to have me taken out so she could have him to herself. Luckily she was the one bitch in the Roc he has no desire to fuck."

She got up and moved next to me and held me. "Mya, she tried to call out to you, she tried to save you. It was just too late. She loved you, she just hated me. You don't have to worry about her anymore." I sobbed into my cousins arms because all of this was just overwhelming.

"I just want Tsunami. Why isn't he here? I need him and he isn't here." I cried for a while longer my cousin sat there patiently rubbing my back. Finally lifting my head up I realized my body was sore and I now had a migraine. Hugging Xa one more time I got up to walk her to the door. I could barely walk but I pushed myself. I didn't want my cousin to have to baby my ass.

"You sure you ok," Xa asked one more time?

"Yea I'm good. I'm sure I will see you tomorrow because you going to want to check on me." I forced a smile and locked the door behind her.

I took a moment to just enjoy being out of the hospital. Finally being home felt so good to me. I showered twice getting the hospital smell off my skin. I took my pain pills and started to feel better. I walked around the quiet house and it was disturbing not hearing anything at all. I missed hearing Tamir's baby talk but at least I knew he was safe with his daddy. I was so stressed about Tamir being hurt that I never had time to feel the relief of knowing Tsunami was his father and not Creek .I just got home but I was sure they would both be here soon enough. Tsunami had never let me down. Grabbing the remote I put on some mindless reality show and curled up on the couch. I would just relax a little until my man and baby came back to me.

I must have fallen asleep because I woke up to a completely dark house and a cramp in my neck. "Tsu," I called out but my voice just came back to me with no other response. Hearing a knock on the door I slowly got up and went to answer. I felt a little apprehensive since Xa never said anything about Malik being caught or taken care of so I had no idea if I was still a target. Looking out the window next to my door I pulled the curtain back slowly. A tall white blonde lady with some Winnie the Pooh scrubs on stood there with a stethoscope around her neck.

Swinging the door opened I tried not to let my attitude show. "Can I help you," I said my voice sharp with anger? I wanted Tsunami not a fucking nurse.

She looked a little shocked at how rude I was being but all fucking well. "Umm Mister Merrick sent me over to be your nurse for the next six weeks." She was nervous and stumbling over her words. I stood there feeling my heart drop. Oh that's how this dirty nigga wanted to act. Like what the fuck did I do to him? He can't come home and take care of me.

"Tell Mister Merrick I said FUCK YOU," I said slamming the door in her face. I turned off my phone and made sure to put the chain lock on my door. I didn't want to be bothered with anyone today. Grabbing the bottle of Alize I had on the counter I made myself a drink. I didn't care if I wasn't supposed to mix the shit with pain pills. I was going to do whatever I wanted for once in my life. Pulling out my laptop I checked in on my online Avon business and then submitted letters to my professors explaining my situation. I noticed Tsunami's Black card on the dresser and decided to treat myself.

By the time the sun was going down I had ordered thousands in clothes, shoes, pots and pans and even toys for Tamir. I was buying shit just to buy it. I fell asleep with the computer opened to Amazon. I woke up alone again. I tried to call Tsunami but he sent me to voicemail. Fuck him I told myself. I got up and forced myself to move around. I was already receiving some of my packages that came through Prime so I made room for my new stuff. This became my new routine, I woke up every day and did the same shit. I started taking walks and doing some light work outs because I didn't want to get fat just sitting around. I couldn't wait to go back to school next month. For now I was doing all my work from home.

Out of boredom I had been talking to Haze more since he was the only nigga fucking with me. I even started letting him come over and hang out with me. I had become so lonely some days I couldn't eat or sleep. It was making me sick. I was missing Tsunami as my man but I was missing him more as my best friend. He had always been there in my space in my life until now. He just disappeared with no explanation. He sent Tamir home with Xanaya and a detailed custody agreement. I would have my son four days a week and he had him the other three days. Xanaya or Scar would pick Tamir up and bring him to his father. I literally had been texting him for weeks and no response. I didn't get him at all.

Flopping on the couch I opened my Ben & Jerrys Cherry Garcia ice cream and started tearing that shit up. I swear this baby stayed giving me cravings. Hearing my door creek I jumped up scared. "What the fuck you scared for Mya," Tsunami said walking in looking good as fuck. He was so damn cocky. His dreads were down hanging and he had on a long sleeved Balmain shirt and a pair of Balmain jeans. They hung slightly off his ass and I could see his plaid boxers. I could smell the Gucci Guilty cologne from across the room. My pussy was jumping. "You deaf now, can't speak? Shit you been calling every day Kahmya what the fuck you want," he asked in a rude tone?

"Why are you doing this Tsu? I didn't do shit to you but you just abandoned me in the hospital and then ignore me like all these years we been putting in meant nothing." I felt my lip wobble but I held those tears in because I couldn't let life keep beating me down. "You know what Tsunami, fuck it if you don't want me just be man enough to come out and say it. Don't stand there with your attitude playing mind games. You don't want a bitch to call you anymore fuck it I won't. It's other niggas I can call. I'm done." I almost knocked him over as I ran upstairs to my room and slammed the door. Fuck these niggas.

Tsunami

I watched Mya run up the stairs and sighed. I didn't know what the fuck I was doing where she was concerned. I didn't know why I was treating shorty like shit. I just had a hard time getting over my son being hurt. If she would have let me take that test he would have never been in harm's way to begin with. I still loved her ass though. Seeing her for the first time in a long while had me feeling some kind of way. I sat just sat in the house looking out the window for the longest. I know she said she wasn't about to cry but I heard her sobbing for hours upstairs until it was silent.

Hearing a knock on the door I got up and answered that shit. As the door swung open my gun met that bitch made nigga Haze before he could even ask for my shorty. "Nah nigga aint shit here for you son, don't come back to my shit again." He stared me down for not saying anything but I could see the defiance in his eyes. Pulling back the clip he nodded his head an moved off the steps. He tried to move slow like he was confident but I could tell he was shook. She tripping having this pussy come here like this wasn't still my shit.

Running up the stairs I flung the bedroom door open but stopped when I saw Mya curled up in the middle of the bed. Her hand was resting over her belly and her long hair hung framing her face. She looked cold because for some reason she was on the covers and not under them. She had on a pair of pink boy shorts and a cream tank top. Her breasts had gotten bigger from the pregnancy and that shit had my dick rocked up. Pulling back the covers I took off my jeans, shirt and Timbs before I turned off the lights. Snatching her ass up I pulled her closer and started sucking on her neck. Her eyes popped open in shock, "Tsu what the fuck are you doing," she asked? I could tell she wanted to have an attitude but couldn't.

"Shhh," I said before I pulled up her shirt and took her swollen nipple in my mouth. Her whole body shuddered with pleasure and her back arched. I took my time and kissed every inch of her body. Looking at the scars still red and raw from her getting shot it pissed me off all over again. I should have prevented this shit somehow. On some level I felt hurt that my sister was dead but I also felt regret that I didn't get to kill her. She caused me to almost lose the person in my life that meant the most. Letting my hands take control I found her fat pussy dripping wet. "Come ride this dick baby," I said sliding her boy shorts off. She didn't fight me at all she hopped on my dick and started moving her waist in a circle. I almost lost my mind her shit was so tight.

I lay back with my eyes low just watching her do her thing. She was playing with her titties and riding my dick like it was about to run away if she aint stay on it. I could feel her gripping me as she came her face was bawled up with a look of pleasure. Not being able to take it anymore I slapped her as before flipping her over. I gently grabbed her leg and put it on my shoulder. Looking down at her sloppy wet pussy I knew I wasn't going to make it. "Shit, girl this pussy is so fucking good," I said hitting her spot harder I made her shit cream again. I thought about the fact that I was the first nigga to ever slide up in her and bust the biggest nut ever.

She sat on her side looking at me and I knew she wanted to talk or some bullshit but I wasn't in the mood. Thinking about the way Haze just invited himself over in the middle of the night pissed me off. I bit the shit out of her exposed nipple and she yelped. "Oww, Tsunami that shit hurt." I turned my back on her trying to control my temper. I wanted to slam her ass to the ground and ask her why she fucking with another nigga. She had never seen that side of me before and I swear I was trying my best to hold it. "That's it you fuck me and turn your back. Tsunami get the fuck out," she said shoving me from behind.

I moved so fast she damn near jumped out of the bed. "Mya Iaint going no fucking where until I'm ready," I grabbed her by her hair and pulled her face to mine. That shit with Haze is dead, I don't want to see that nigga around you no more. You got a day to figure that shit out." I couldn't read the look on her face because it was one I had never seen before. Suddenly her hand came flying out of nowhere and something hard bashed me in the face. My hand let go of her hair as she tried to hit me again with the remote control. "Yo B you fucking crazy, you don't think I won't whoop yo little ass in here." I saw blood dripping onto the comforter and I wanted to laugh because this wasn't like Mya.

She kicked me in the side, "I said get the fuck out, no I aint crazy and you aint whooping shit over here. I will fight your ass. You think the shit you could do to me with your hands could even compare to the way you have fucked up my heart. You ignore me treat me like fuck me then you want to roll up in here and beat up the pussy now you issuing demands. This my shit so don't come back here anymore until you learn to act right and this joint custody shit is dead. I'm the fucking mother so bring me my son. You can visit him when I feel like it. If you can't love me cool I will move on but you will respect me." She threw the remote at me and walked to the bathroom. That didn't go how I thought it would.

Throwing my clothes on I grabbed a hand towel to wipe the blood from my face. Jogging down the stairs I made my way to the black Maxima with the blacked out tints I been riding in. I sat in the car and reclined the seat. Glancing in the mirror over the windshield I laughed to myself as I saw the cut above my eyebrow. Mya straight got my ass, I guess my guard wasn't up because I never thought she would swing on ya boy. Putting my chrome nine on my lap I went right back to doing what I been doing since Mya ass been home, watching her crib.

Chapter 9 – Crossing All the Lines

Xanaya

I was now five months pregnant and finally going to see if I was having a girl or a boy today, I could have found out weeks ago but I was meeting Mya and we were going together. I was praying for a girl because this was it for a while. I didn't want to be one of these young girls stuck at home with a whole bunch of fucking small kids and no life. Or worse end up financially struggling because I got a gaggle of babies running behind me. Scar wouldn't care either way because he always thought this drug shit was going to last forever but look at what happened to Nazia and he wasn't even in the game. At any time you could be caught slipping and if he got caught up or killed I had to still be a mother to mine. But men didn't think about shit like that.

I rolled over and Scar ass was still snoring, a little drool spot had formed on the pillow next to his face and I hurried to grab my phone. Using my thumbprint I unlocked it and took a three second video of this shit. He swore he didn't snore at all. I leaned over and kissed him on the cheek, then the neck and worked my way to his lips. I kissed him deep, morning breath and all. He opened one eye and smirked at me. Looking at his rock hard dick had me sliding my horny as back under the sheets. I let my hands roam all over his chest until I found the head of his dick. Gently squeezing I began jacking him off as he sucked my breasts. I knew I had to hurry before his blocking ass son woke up. Gently I shoved him onto his back and I slid my way up his body.

Sliding my silk thong to the side I shuddered when I felt his length penetrate me. I swear I will never get used to his size. I was creaming right away ready to cum all over but he lifted my hips taking away my sex candy. I struggled whining against the head which was all he let me have trying to force him to put it back in. "Scar come on baby give me what I want. I need the dick," I begged. As soon as he slammed me back on his dick I rode it like it was the last time. I hopped up so I was crouching on my feet and began twerking on the head then dropped it like it was hot. "BAM BAM BAM," someone was banging on the door like the police. Looking around to make sure Scar didn't have any guns or weed lying around everything looked fine.

"SCYIONY GET YOUR ASS OUT HERE," Shelly's annoying voice screeched reaching all the way upstairs to the bedroom. See this shit wasn't going to fly today. I jumped up with my white thong only on and ran my ass downstairs. Belly and titties out I didn't give a fuck, I was so tired of this hoe. Calling all day and night, always trying to use her son as some reason to come around. Yanking the door open so hard my arm instantly began to hurt I caught her fist mid bang. Shoving her ass backwards so hard she flew down the stairs and damn near landed on her son. I followed her outside and grabbed the nearest branch I could find. It had a knot on the end and I picked it up and whapped the shit out of her side a few times.

"Xanaya, what the fuck are you doing," Scar said disbelief in his voice. His neighbors were outside watching me with nothing on but a patch of silk and our sex juices running down my legs. He tried to grab me but I punched him in the face. I was getting tired of this shit. She stayed in her place as the ultimate side bitch for years now she was everywhere.

"I'm out here doing what the fuck you should have been doing. Controlling this fucking dog ass hoe." He forcefully pushed me in the house pinching my arm hard as a bitch. I didn't give a fuck about him being pissed off. That was exactly why I was going back to my crib I didn't have to fucking be here.

"Xanaya at least put clothes on if you going to whoop her ass. You out here putting on a fucking World Star Video for the neighborhood like a common hood rat," he said looking stressed out. Little did he know his stress was just beginning. His son was crying and reaching for his mother who mushed him in the face and began dusting herself off.

"Shut up lil crying ass nigga, that's why I'm here matter of fact. Shit if you not going to fuck me or be with me you can have his ass. I been doing this shit for almost three years and I'm good. His papers are in the plastic bag he's holding, don't fucking call me. Oh he allergic to some shit but I can't fucking remember," she got up and hopped in her broke down as Honda and pulled away. Poor Kevon stood there confused, his little lip quivered and tears zig zagged down his face.

I ran out and grabbed him in my arms, making sure to bump the shit out of Scar on my way in. "Dumb ass nigga, look at the woman you cheat with. Who abandons their son," I asked not really expecting an answer. I took off his jacket and stripped him from the filthy ass clothes he had on. Carrying him to the bathroom I ran a bubble bath putting some of Favours toys in the tub. Scar followed behind me like a lost ass puppy dog. I bet his ass was speechless for once. Watching a mother do some shit like that would leave anyone speechless. Fuck if I sneezed he was choking me or manhandling my ass but this hoe treats his son like an unwanted animal and he's just standing there stuck on stupid. Maybe I had to rethink this relationship shit with him. I knew that things had been going to well.

"Get him a towel and some clothes you just standing there. Do something shit," I said my temper on a thousand. I had taken the two raggedy ass braids she had in his head out and washed his hair twice. This shit was child neglect at its finest. Shaking my head I began talking to him about Paw Patrol trying to take his mind off the shit he been going through. A second later a towel hit me dead in my face. "Ole fuck nigga," I yelled as he walked back to the other room. "I gotta go so pack him a bag of clothes, the ones we keep here so he can go to your grandma's house with King."

I took him out and rubbed him down with Johnson and Johnson. Snatching the gray and green Gap sweat suit out of Scars hands I dressed him fast. He hadn't said a word since he came inside his brown eyes were wide open like he was scared. I made sure to give him an extra hug and kiss so he knew he was good. "Naw he good I will keep him with me today," he said coming around the corner. Tilting my head to the side I watched as he stood there with a sneaky ass look on his face.

"Scar don't play with me, hand me the grease and comb from the dresser and go find some clothes. You know we have a doctor's appointment." He handed me the stuff and had a crazy look on his face as he went to get dressed. I was glad his ass aint say shit else to me because I was ready to start swinging on him and it was too early. After plaiting three neat braids in Kevon's hair I picked him up and made my way to the car. "SCAR we in the fucking car let's go, and nigga you driving," I yelled slamming the front door. With this pregnancy I hated driving or really doing anything but sleeping in and eating.

He slid in the driver's seat of the car looking like the cat had ate his homework. Really I didn't care. The drive over was silent, not even Kevon made any noise. Turning to look at him I noticed he was sleeping, his head resting against the side of the car seat his hands folded in his lap. "Scar don't you let this bitch get him back. Take a DNA test and then get custody."

"Why you always talking about a fucking DNA test ma, you really got some nerve trying to push a fucking test on me. Remember when your punk ass wouldn't even give me one for King." I looked at him with hate in my eyes. How the fuck does that compare to this, I thought there was zero chance that he was the father. I wasn't trying to pin a kid on him so why didn't he understand that was different. "Right I see you stuck on fucking mute right," he asked egging me on? "Don't mention that shit anymore, this my son so shut the fuck up about some DNA."

Looking at him in disbelief I didn't even respond. Scar was going to lose me again and the next time would be for good. I didn't want to keep running from him and doing the back and forth shit so for the moment I was going to try with him. I had to grow up and not always jump and act a fool. But believe the DNA subject wasn't over by a long shot.

Scar

Pulling up to my Grams house I knew this shit was going to be messy. She didn't know I had another son and I wasn't looking forward to her reaction. I wanted to slow the process of us getting out of the car down but it seemed like Xa knew I was up to something since she jumped out of the car and grabbed Kevon. I slowly trailed behind her as she walked inside. "Hey baby, whose this," my grandma asked her with a curious look on her face.

"Grams what do you mean who is this, it's Kevon. Don't you recognize him," Xa asked before they both turned to look at me. "Really Scar, even for you this is a new low. You didn't tell her about your son? I knew you kept him a secret from me, but your grandmother," Xanaya really looked disgusted with me. I never did the right by her and every day shit seemed to get worse and worse. I didn't tell my Grams about Kevon because a part of me really didn't think he was mine and another part of me knew she wouldn't lie to Xa for me. I felt like shit but I couldn't change the past.

"Lil nigga I swore I raised you to be better than this. You hiding babies and shit," grams cussed me the fuck out then slapped the shit out of the back of my head. Her old ass could hit, her hand felt like a two ton brick. Wincing I didn't say anything because there was nothing to say. "Naw speak up, say something you wan't to stand over there looking like a sad puppy dog. That don't work anymore, you're a whole grown ass man so act like one."

"Look Grams you right I'm a man. I cheated on Xa

back in the day with some little hoe in school. She ended up getting pregnant but I just kept it on the low because I knew it would break Xanaya's heart. I'm sure she don't believe it but she's my priority, my life line and it tears me apart every time I hurt her." I looked up to see my grandmother rubbing Xa back. She stood there crying silently. I didn't know what to say because she looked broken and I knew I was the one who broke her. She was tired of my shit and she had other shit going on. With her being pregnant it was just too much. Grabbing Kevon and handing him off to my Grams I held Xa in my arms letting her get her feelings out. "Damn ma I'm sorry, I can say that a million times and I know it doesn't change shit. But please forgive a nigga because I'm nothing without you," I begged kissing her softly.

"Scar I'm really trying," was all she said before slowly walking to the car.

"Grams I'm out," I said hugging her and kissing Kevon. I was glad Favour little ass aint come see us because he would have been crying to come too. Getting in the car I wiped Xa tears. "Come on ma don't cry, it's going to be alright. I got you and I'm not fucking up like that again, I promise." Once I said it I swore I didn't know if it was true. It seemed like I was addicted to bullshit and bullshit usually came in the form of some random girls pussy. Driving to Highland Hospital I pulled in the garage and watched Xa for a few minutes. She had fallen asleep and she looked so peaceful. Maybe because it was the only time she wasn't cussing me out. I gently shook her awake knowing the peace and quiet was about to end.

"What Scar," she snapped annoyed at being woken up or maybe at me touching her. "

"We here get your ass up," I swear I couldn't talk nice to her ass she just annoyed the fuck out of me. But I couldn't live without her. It was like a puzzle that I couldn't figure out. She cut her pretty ass eyes at me but didn't say shit else. Just walked her sexy ass to the door not even looking to see if I was coming or not. They called us back pretty fast and had Xanaya lay back on the table. She pulled up her shirt and I smiled, I loved looking at her pregnant with my seed. I missed out on this shit with Favour but I wouldn't with this baby.

The tech poured some blue shit on her belly and started moving a plastic thing over her belly. Images of my baby came up on the screen and I felt my heart race. "Do you want to know the sex of the baby," she asked?

"Hell yea," I said causing Xanaya to frown. "Girl fix yo damn face, imma be me no matter what," I told her smirking showing off my grills. I wasn't bout to pretend to be some bouijee ass dude just because we was at the doctor's office. The tech didn't care because she had been eyeing me the whole time with a please fuck me face on.

"Ok, well it looks like you will be having a girl," she said causing me to feel faint. I had two boys but a girl was something else. I didn't even know how to handle the way I was feeling. I was going to make sure she was always good, that no niggas fucked with her. No one was going to love my daughter the way I would.

*****

I had been bringing my ass in the house every night and staying out these others bitches wet wet but Xanaya wasn't giving a nigga a fucking break still. Kevon's bitch ass mom hadn't looked back since the day she left him so Xa been playing mommy and was doing a great job. She just wouldn't let up on the DNA test shit. I wanted to snap her fucking neck the way she kept nagging me about it. It made a nigga not even want to come home. "Xa, where you at ma," I called out as I walked into the kitchen. She made one of my favorite's fried chicken, baked beans and mac n cheese. I sat down and ate my food in silence. Shit it was only eight at night but I hadn't heard anything since I came in. I knew Xa was here because her car was outside. Washing my dishes I made my way upstairs and found Xanaya knocked out in our bed with Kevon on one side and Favour on the other. I took out my phone and snapped a picture, it felt like some weak shit to be doing but my love for my family made me not give a fuck.

I put the kids in their beds and took a shower. All I wanted to do was lay up under my girl maybe slide in her wet pussy and get some rest. I got on the bed and pulled her little pajama shirt up and started rubbing her belly. "Hey daddy's girl," I said feeling her kick my hand I smiled. I wasn't going to be like my pops, I wasn't ever leaving my kids. I closed my eyes and thought about how I wanted my future to look. I must have been tired because I drifted off to sleep.

Xanaya

I woke up to see Scar snoring and his hand on my stomach. I could tell he was going to be different with his daughter than he was with his sons. Since he found out it was a girl he had been all up under me. I had been trying to deal with Scar differently than in the past. I made a choice to not run away from him anymore but I was going to clear up this other baby momma shit right away. I crept out of the bed and went in the bathroom to empty my bladder. I brushed my teeth and checked on the kids.

I made sure he was still sleeping before I went in my purse and pulled out the at home DNA kit I ordered the other day. Shoving the swab and vial under my pillow I pulled his monster sized dick out and put it in my mouth. He groaned grabbing my short hair shoving himself to the back of my throat. I made sure to relax my throat and let him slid further in so his whole dick was in my mouth. I made sure to rub his balls at the same time until he just couldn't take it anymore. "Fuck girl, you sucking the shit out of my dick," he got out before he bust.

I didn't began kissing up his chest until I got to his neck were I bit him lightly. "I want you to fuck the shit out of me," I whispered in his ear. I could feel his dick get hard immediately. I knew this was my chance so I had to make it count. "Babe close your eyes," I instructed as I ran my hands all over his body. I knew he loved when I took control and I was going to give him all that he enjoyed. I turned around and squatted on his dick popping my pussy causing his whole body to tense up. Before he could lose his mind

I spun around and kissed his chest while dropping my wet pussy on is dick. As soon as he looked like he couldn't take it anymore and had his mouth slightly open I grabbed the swab and jabbed it in his mouth.

"What the fuck Xa," he yelled damn near tossing my little ass to the floor. He moved quick but I move quicker, I got what I needed from his ass. Not waiting around to deal with the consequences I grabbed my purse threw the vial with the swab inside and ran. I knew Scar was going to fuck my little ass up so I was going to go to my house for a few days and let him cool off. I grabbed a robe on my way out and threw my feet into some slippers.

I snuck in Favours room and snatched him up. I heard Scar laughing upstairs but I didn't know if it was an evil imma fuck you up kind of laugh or a you got me ha ha kind. Not taking any chance I continued outside. Putting the baby into his car seat the fastest I ever have I slid into my car naked as fuck and prayed I didn't get pulled over. I stopped at a drive through Fed Ex and dropped the samples in the box so it was a done deal.

I picked up my phone to call my cousin. "Kahmya, come stay with me tonight I snuck and did a DNA test on Scar while we was fucking and he probably going to come and fuck me up. So come and have girl's night, please," I whined into the phone.

"Ok I will meet you at your house. I hope there is ice-cream," she said before hanging up. Shit I didn't know if I did. I opened my window a little and sang along to the radio as I drove in only a bathrobe. I didn't even know the words to the song I was just making up shit. For the moment I was happy, feeling the adrenaline rush from the stunt I just pulled.

I parked and was happy none of Scars vehicles where parked in my driveway. As soon as I made it to the door Mya was pulling in behind me. "Hurry up I gotta pee," she said hopping around from foot to foot. As soon as we made it inside I put Favour in his bed. I wandered back downstairs to the kitchen opened the fridge and frowned. I had been at Scars house for a while and I had nothing to eat. Two pregnant people and no food that wasn't going to work, shit.

"Where the hell is your clothes," Mya asked eyeing my open bathrobe and slippers?

"Girl long story, I have to go to the store so make a list of what you want." I went in my bedroom and threw on a panties and bra set. Then I went in the bathroom to take a hoe bath and brush my teeth. Feeling lazy I threw on a hoodie and some tights before getting ready to run to the Walmart around the corner. Grabbing my keys I found Mya on the couch curled up with my throw blanket. "Mya listen out for Favour I will be right back. Text me what you want," I called out as I grabbed her keys, "I'm taking your car because your blocking me in."

"Don't crash my shit," she yelled back. I loved my cousin. I sped to Walmart just wanting to get back in the house and eat junk food. Racing my cart up and down the aisles I bought three different flavors of ice-cream including the strawberry I had been craving. I threw Oreos, frozen pizzas and pickles in the mix. Soon the cart was too heavy to push so I cashed out. I looked around me for once not feeling like I was being followed. Breathing a sigh of relief I loaded all of my groceries in the car and drove home. Pulling in the driveway I hoped Mya ass didn't fall asleep on me because all the lights were off.

I got to the door and realized I didn't have a house key because I had her keys. I knocked on the front door but it flew open. What the fuck. "MYA," I called out as I slowly walked in. My foot landed in something wet and sticky. Using the flashlight on my phone I looked down to see what I stepped in and noticed the blood. I felt so much fear I dropped my phone. Flicking on the lights I noticed the house looked like someone had ransacked the place and Mya was nowhere in sight. I knew Scar didn't do this, someone else had been here. Running upstairs to Favours room I tripped on the stairs twice. After what seemed like forever I reached his room. I opened the door and saw that his crib was empty.

Chapter 10 - Damsel in Distress

Kahmya

Looking at Malik as he paced back and forth I wasn't even scared anymore. I hadn't cried the whole time, not when he hit me in the shoulder with the gun to get me to shut up or even when he tied my wrists so tight my hands went numb. All I could focus on was making sure Favour was ok. My cousin was all I had besides my kids and Sarai and I would never let anyone hurt her son. The house I was being held in was the same house Malik used to live in with his mom and sister when we all went to school together but since I was being held hostage in the middle of the living room I'm assuming that they had long since moved out.

Inside from what I could see was kind of bare. No pictures on the walls, just white paint. Aside from a really odd smell it was clean, freakishly clean, the blankets on the end of the couches were folded into perfect squares and the few pieces of mail on the coffee table appeared to be in a perfect pile. This didn't stop Malik from stopping to straighten them all over again. When Favour dropped crumbs from his cookie onto the couch he was there with a small vacuum cleaning them up. He had a look of pure rage on his face and I felt my body stiffen waiting on him to even look at Favour funny. I was going to find a way to fuck him all the way up.

I was not tied up for the moment because he needed me to hold the baby so he could hold is gun. I pulled Favour closer to me and tried to settle him down hoping he would fall asleep. I had to use my head and find a way out of this fucking place. Malik began talking to himself as he continued to peak out of the curtains. "Where are you? I know you're coming for your son. What kind of mother are you XANAYA," he screamed and began banging his fists on the wall. "I have the candy you love and the roses you love waiting on you. Don't keep your man waiting. Our son is ready for our new life together." He glanced at Favour then with a lost look in his eyes. He was smiling but it wasn't right. Not like I needed any more confirmation that he was bat shit crazy.

Favour started to cry a little and his head shot up like he was coming too. "Shut him up," he snarled. I immediately began rocking him, trying to make my body relax so he would do the same. After a few more minutes he shoved his face in my breasts and fell asleep. Exhaling a sigh of relief I closed my eyes for a moment to say a little prayer. "Bitch why you over there looking so fucking satisfied? You like this rough shit or you just stupid? Do you know why I took you?" He stood there waiting for a few minutes waiting on an answer. I slowly shook my head no. "You are my insurance policy, I know Xanaya is coming for you and when I have her then I won't need your ass anymore. If you're a good girl I won't make you suffer like the others, I will end it quickly."

His words should have struck fear in my heart instead it just made me furious. I was so fucking tired of being a victim. This shit with Creek, my mother, Haze and even Tsunami. I felt courage flow through my veins as I decided to not even entertain his nonsense for the moment. I discreetly began looking around the areas I could see and try to think of a weapon I could use. Malik went back to talking to himself and pacing the floors. We continued on that way until the early hours of the morning. My left arm was almost numb from holding on to Favour but I wouldn't dare put my baby cousin down around this monster. I

He never fell asleep or even began to look sleepy. I wondered if he was on something or just high on life. "Malik I know I'm your prisoner but can you grab me something to eat. Some noodles, crackers something? Just so I can remain alive until Xanaya comes here." His head jerked around and his eyes narrowed. He didn't answer one way or the other just used a key to make sure the locks on the front door were locked and slowly walked to the kitchen. I heard the fridge open and the microwave start up. Something smelled good, maybe Chinese food.

"Here," he said shoving a bowl of shrimp low mien into my free hand. I was starving because Tsunami's baby had no respect for situations and was demanding to eat. I picked up the fork and began to eat trying not to choke on the food. God knows this niggas wasn't going to save me if I did. As soon as I finished the food he came over and snatched the bowl out of my hand. I didn't even think about what I was doing as I took the fork and jabbed it into his neck. At first it felt like I had really fucked up because the fork barely broke the skin but I found strength and shoved harder. Pulling it out I immediately rammed it back in this time I must have struck something because blood squirted everywhere. I could see the shocked look on Malik's face, his eyes were wide in shock and his body was rigid. The empty glass bowl he had in his hand dropped and crashed to the hard wood floor shattering on impact.

He tried to turn his hand with the gun towards me but I lifted my foot and kicked him in the side. All the anger I felt from people trying to ruin my life and hurt me was in that kick. He flew across the floor and hit his head on the end table. I jumped up as fast as I could with Favour on my side. I was pissed when I got to the front door and forgot it was locked from the inside. Racing to the back I could see a door that was connected to the basement. Fuck. I heard Malik groaning and thrashing around so I knew he wasn't dead, yet.

Opening the basement door I was thankful that was not locked. Taking the stairs carefully since it was dark I fumbled for a light switch once I hit the bottom stairs. As soon as it flickered on I wanted to turn that shit right back off. The sight before me had me totally floored. I was just standing there in shock, thoughts of escaping had left me, hell even breathing had left me. A young blonde woman or what was left of her was tied to some dentists looking chair in front of me. Her eye lids where peeled away and her tongue was cut out. Her silent screams gave me goosebumps and caused me to piss on myself. Beyond her was piled of bodies in neat rows. Some were intact and others where just piles of bones.

Feeling the bile rise in my throat I glanced at the young girl again. I swear she wanted me to help her by the look in her blue eye balls but I knew I had to get the fuck out of there. Turning around I went back where I came from and looked around to make sure Malik hadn't moved far. He was on his side clutching his neck with blood seeping through his fingers. Thinking quick I picked up a chair from the kitchen and threw it at the front window. Glass flew all over the front lawn and I made my way to climb out. Even while on the floor dying he was trying to crawl his way towards me. I wanted to stop and spit in his face but remembering the girl in the basement I decided I should go and get some help.

I cut my bare feet once I climbed out of the window. I couldn't stop shivering from the cold air on my damn near bare skin. This nigga snatched me in some tiny ass pajama shorts and a tank top. Favour was wide awake now and crying, he kept wiggling trying to get down so he could crawl around not understanding what was going on. At least he had on warm footie pajamas and a blanket. Running to the nearest neighbor's house I banged on the door repeatedly until it was flung open. "Why the hell are you banging on my fucking door," the middle aged black lady cussed me out before the door was fully opened. Looking me over she stopped and whipped out her cell phone.

"Are you ok," she asked as she put nine one one on speaker phone. I broke down crying as she led me into her house and locked the door.

"I need to call my cousin please so she can come and get me and so she knows we are ok. This is her baby and we were kidnapped," I explained fast hoping she would let me get one phone call so I could get the fuck out of here before the police came. I was a victim but I still killed a man. Handing me the phone I tried Xanaya but she never picked up. Not knowing anyone else's number by heart besides Tsunami I tried him.

"Yo who the fuck is this," he said his deep voice sounded aggravated like he was in the middle of something.

"Tsunami it's me, please come and get me," I cried into the receiver.

"Mya where are you, I'm on my way ma. We been looking everywhere for you. Are you ok," he asked in a panic? After telling him the address I sat in a chair and waited. Resting my bloody feet on a white towel until I could get to a hospital I clung on to Favour and counted my blessings. I swear I was like a cat with nine lives. Finally I heard a knock on the door and Tsunami was running into the room squeezing the breath out of me. Xanaya and Scar were not far behind. Once again I ended up in a hospital but not overnight.

The police questioned me for hours asking me a lot of questions I didn't have answers too. Apparently Malik wasn't just a woman beater or a nigga obsessed with my cousin he was a psychopath. Some of those bodies he had in his basement were girls we went to school with who we had assumed just quit school. Others were just random women he grabbed from public places. I wasn't surprised when the police informed us that his mother and sister were among the piles of bones in the basement.

Tsunami hadn't left my side the entire time but I wasn't sure why. He made it clear he wasn't fucking wit me since I was shot. "Tsu you can go, I'm sure you got shit to do and I can Uber or whatever." He looked at me like I told him his dick was on fire.

"Kahmya shut up and sign these papers so we can go home. And I don't want to hear shit about that nigga Haze unless you want him to end up like those niggas in Malik basement. Missing eyelids and fingernails, straight slaughtered. I didn't bother telling him I had kicked Haze in the nuts after I spit in his face months ago. We had been over before he decided to try and lay down the law. I just rolled my eyes and went back to my release papers, even though it made me feel good having Tsu next to me.

On our way to my house he stopped at Sarai's to pick up Tamir. I was so happy to see my son, I thought of him the whole time I was being held. Him and Favour were the people who gave me the strength to get away. I knew I was making it home to my son. I crawled in the backseat and sat next to his car seat. He kept smacking me in the face and calling out "Dada," but I didn't even care. I kissed his chubby cheeks and ran my hand through his curls. Finally I got my "Mama," as he gave me a sloppy baby kiss. Putting my hand on my belly I felt my daughter kick hard and I knew she could feel my joy. I didn't know how to tell my family and Tsunami this but I was leaving New York and taking my kids with me. Fuck a court judge and a lawyer I wasn't leaving my babies. I had to get the fuck out of here.

Tsunami

I went crazy when Mya went missing. I tore through the city killing everyone I could think of that had anything to do with this shit. If I didn't kill them Scar did. We now had more enemies than ever due to kicking in doors, fucking up the blocks and peoples operations. Hearing her voice today made me feel so much relief. I ran every red light getting to the address she gave me. Once I made sure her and Favour was ok I had all intentions of going to kill Malik. But walking in to find him dead on the floor, a fork sticking out of his neck let me know that Mya handled that for me. I was just happy she got away. I saw the state of the women in the basement and a chill ran down my back. He was torturing bitches like this was an episode of Crime Scene Investigation.

I didn't say too much to Mya until I pulled up in my driveway. "Tsunami why are we here," she asked exhaustion in her voice. I didn't want her back at her house and I sure as fuck wasn't leaving her alone. Not another day ever in life was she going to be without me. She just didn't know. I didn't respond at first, I opened the back door and picked up Tamir.

"Come on ma, hush, I got you My," I said helping her out of the car. She didn't argue just leaned on me a little. I think she missed me as much as I missed her. Once we got inside I got Tamir ready for bed, "babe go shower," I told her throwing a towel her way. I had Sarai bring her some clothes when we were at the hospital so I motioned towards her bag in the corner.

She slowly walked in and I heard the water turn on. Stripping down to my boxers I decided to give her some space and stay out the bathroom. I didn't even put Tamir in his bed because I was sure she didn't want to be far from him tonight. She walked out naked and I could see the curve of her baby belly. My heart filled with love for her and my seed. Mya went to my dresser and found a t-shirt and put it on ignoring her clothes except to grab a pair of panties.

She crawled in the bed next to me and pulled Tamir close. I covered them up and turned the TV on before I went to handle my hygiene. I took my time in the bathroom. I made a few calls and shaved the beard I had let grow since I had only been focused on getting my girl back. Finally I jumped in the steaming hot shower and let the water ease the tension in my body. A part of me felt like less of a man because I didn't get rid of the people who hurt Mya. She handled Malik, Chania didn't stand a chance against Xanaya and neither did Kimora. All I could do now was take care of her and show her I loved her. Maybe I would kill that bitch ass nigga Haze just because.

Walking into the bedroom I could see her eyes shining in the light from the television. "Ma what's up, why you not asleep," I asked with worry in my voice. In the car she could barely hold up her head but here she was still wide awake. She shrugged but I saw a look pass over her face. Not pushing I climbed into bed behind her and pulled her into my chest. She rested her head on my arm and intertwined her fingers in mine. "Kahmya you know I love you. When you were gone I never stopped looking. I haven't slept since the moment Scar told me what happened. I made this bitch bleed and would have kept on if you didn't save yourself."

She lightly kissed my arm and curled her body deeper in mine so I knew she was listening. "Mya I'm sorry ma, to think I could ever live without you was crazy. I shouldn't have forced you to have this baby when you were going through so much. I should have been listening to you."

"It's a girl," she said low.

"What," I asked barely hearing her.

"This baby, it's a girl, we are going to have a daughter in five months." She rolled over to look at me.

"Wow My, how long have you known? And why didn't you say shit to me," I asked running my hand over her cheek. I was pissed but didn't want to act like an asshole. She had been going through too much to have to put up with my selfish ass attitude.

"Tsu you had basically said fuck me. I didn't even think you wanted this baby anymore. You didn't come home from the hospital with me you didn't fuck with me at all. Except the one time you blessed me with some dick then crept out of the house in the middle of the night like a bitch. When you dropped off Tamir after that you wouldn't even look in my face so I just didn't say shit. Plus I had just found out a few days before I was kidnapped. I would have told you I'm sure. I'm weak for you, always have been." She laughed up at me when she said that. Her smile made me fall in love with her all over again. My body was reacting to having her so close but I was telling my man to chill. No way was I making this shit about sex. That's some Scar and Xa shit, what we had was deeper.

"You right ma, you got that. I wasn't playing fair or treating you the way you deserved. But don't ever say I aint fuck wit you at all. Shit I spent most of my nights in whip across the street from your crib just looking at this shit. I felt better knowing I was close in case you needed me. Mya I'm always fucking wit you bae, believe that." I let my lips meet hers and kissed her for what felt like the first time in forever. She tasted like mint toothpaste and sweetness. Her mouth was warm as she parted her lips and let her tongue touch mine. I stopped when I tasted her salty tears. "You good," I said causing her to cover her face with her eyes. She was dead ass crying like a baby, body shaking and all.

"Shh, come on its ok you're ok now. I told you I got you. No one's going to hurt you again. Ma it's me and you against the world. No more separate houses or bullshit games. You my woman and that's it, I aint fucking wit nobody else." I rolled on my back pulling her on top of me so her tears wet my chest. I just rubbed her back and waited for her to tell me what was going on in her head.

"Tsu, that's what I've always wanted. I wanted to be your girl for what felt like my whole life. But I have to tell you something and it's not something I can change at this time or compromise on." I said a little prayer that she wasn't about to tell me this baby wasn't mine or no crazy shit like that. I held my breath waiting for her to say what had her so stressed she was crying and shaking. "Tsu I can't stay here, I made that decision the moment I killed him. Too much has happened and I have to get out."

Letting out a sigh of relief I laughed a little. "Girl fuck this house, shit we can buy whatever kind of place you want. I got you, you want to move closer to Sarai we can do that, or near Xanaya? The school? This yo world ma." She leaned on her elbows and I realized she was probably not that comfortable because of the baby. Letting her slid next to me I still held her close.

"No Tsunami, I meant I can't stay in New York. This place has been the epitomy of hell for me. Every place I go leaves a bad memory. I'm stuck thinking abour being raped or beaten half to death. I don't want another child born here. Look at what happened to Tamir. I haven't decided where to go but being here is not an option. I don't want my kids to be raised in a place that has caused us so much pain.

So you see the problem." She put her head down in regret and sadness.

"Shorty look at me, don't put your head down. Kahmya I have loved you the same way, unconditionally since the day I saw you. I have slept in hallways, killed for you and even shed tears behind you. You don't want to stay in New York, cool, fuck a New York. We can be out this bitch as soon as you pick a place. I still have to come here to run my business but I don't have to live her. I'm not a corner nigga anymore and I aint got no one in this fucking world but you and our kids. Scar and Lynk ass know how to fly they can visit and these little niggas can keep holding down the traps. My mom is dead to me and I aint got no other family. You're my family and I will follow you anywhere. Now where you wanna move baby," I asked meaning everything I said?

"Could we move to Miami? That way when Sarai visits Lynk I will still have a friend around? Plus the beaches are pretty and it's so warm. It will be a fresh start for us and we need it." I nodded in agreement and she wound her arms around my neck. "I love you Tsu," she whispered.

"I love you too Mya," I responded with a smile on my face as I rested my hand on her belly and closed my eyes so I could finally get some rest.

Epilogue- Two Years Later
Take a Chance on me
Xanaya

"Kevon come on baby you're going to be late for school," I said shaking him a little. He was a character just like Scar ass, he opened one eye and pulled the covers back up to his face. I didn't know at five years old kids could have fucking jokes. Since my friends moved to Florida my life was all about the kids. Me and Scar were still rocking together but his pattern of cheating and apologizing was getting weak and fast. I had been looking into houses in Miami on the low. I was just going to pack up the kids and leave one day, one day soon.

I hated to disrupt Kevon's school year but I found a good private school and he would adjust, kids always did. Even though he wasn't my flesh and blood he had become my son and I wasn't leaving him behind. His mother was no fucking good, she never looked back after she left him, not a call or text. Not even after Scar told her that he wasn't the father, we tried to call a few weeks later and she had her number changed. So we just made the decision to keep him and raise him ourselves.

I rolled him over and forced him to sit up. He rubbed his hands over his tiny eyes and finally wandered into his bathroom so he could pee. "Kevon your clothes are on the bed get dressed baby," I called out. I double checked that he had socks on his neatly folded clothes because they always ended up forgotten. I had to grab my daughter before she screamed the house down. Patience wasn't her strong suit. Hearing the front door open I glanced at the clock and rolled my eyes. This nigga was never going to change, here it was seven AM and he was just creeping his way in the house. He walked into our room and grabbed some clean boxers and a wife beater. I didn't even bother to speak and neither did he. I was pissed but his punk ass was just guilty.

I had thirty minutes before Kevon's bus came so I settled Sci in her play pen and peaked in on Favour. He was in his bed curled up with his dinosaur pillow mouth wide open. He had never been a morning person. I gently closed his door as Kevon ran into me in the hallway. "Mama can I have pancakes," he asked then smiled. He had both front teeth missing on top so I could see all in his mouth.

Running my hands over his curls I giggled. "Of course you can. Go sit down at the table." I made a stack of pancakes and cut some fresh fruit and made my kids plates. I could smell his body wash and cologne before he came up behind me smacking my ass. I didn't respond in any way I just let my shoulders droop. I hated that I loved him. A man who cheated on me every chance he got. Why wasn't I enough for him? I couldn't even hold on to my anger anymore all I felt was emptiness and sadness.

"You not making your man a plate," he had the nerve to ask? I looked up at him in disbelief as I helped Kevon on with his coat and backpack.

"My man, hell show me that nigga. As a matter of fact, have whoever you just came from make you breakfast. This aint Ihop and I don't work off of tips." Walking my baby to the bus I waved at him as they drove away and tried to hold the smile on my face. I closed the door and rested my head against it trying not to cry. Scar walked over and pulled me into his arms. He started to speak but I just couldn't do it with him anymore. "Please just don't, I can't hear I'm sorry or I'm going to do better one more time. Scar I give up, just let me go. I'm not enough for you, I can respect that but be honest enough to say it and stop hurting me."

We stood there with me sobbing into his chest for a few minutes. "Ding ding ding," my doorbell chimed causing me to jump. I was searching my brain trying to remember if I ordered something online because if not I didn't know who could have been ringing my bell. I looked at him and he just shrugged as confused as I was. Sci started to cry so Scar went to grab her while I answered the door.

A short brown skin girl was standing in front of me. Her short long weave was pulled away from her face in a low ponytail. She had on a red low cut sweater and a pair of jeans. Her red ballet flats were tapping the welcome mat and she had her arms folded like I was the one wasting her time. After a moment of her still just standing there without saying something I decided I would say something. "Can I help you," I asked still lost as fuck. Her pug looking face bawled up even more as she rolled her neck and let her hands fall to her sides.

Stepping forward in an aggressive manner she finally said what she came to say. "Bitch don't act like you don't know who I am. You're fucking my man on the low and I want the shit to stop. No matter what SZA said side chicks aren't winning boo. So this will be your first and only warning about my man."

Bucking my eyes I couldn't believe this bitch was on my doorstep trying to check me about my nigga. The nigga I been fucking, sucking and holding down since high school. "So just for clarity who the fuck is your man?" I could feel my hazel eyes turning darker as my temper made its way to the surface.

"Damn you girls love to play stupid. You know I'm talking about Scar. We have been together almost a year now and I keep seeing your picture pop up in his phone. Around here is not that big so I easily found yo ass. Now what you wanna do bitch because I'm ready to fight for mine." She had her hands clenched in fists and had put one foot forward like a runner getting ready for a race.

"You come to my house, to tell me shit about my man, the one I got three kids wit and I'm the slow bitch. You want Scar ass have him shit because I'm not built for this. I promise one thing though all you ever got from him was a nut and a McDonalds Happy Meal. This house, those cars, he bought all that shit for me and I will always come first, even if we not together." I finished by waving my hands at my candy red Benz truck and cocaine white Porsche. "As a matter of fact hold on your man is home, take his punk ass wit you," I said as I turned to go back inside. "SCIONY," I screamed putting some base in my voice. He came to the door with his hand on his gat and a concerned look on his face. "It's for you," I calmly said as I walked my ass inside to look up moving companies. I was done.

A few minutes later as I sat at the breakfast bar in front of my MacBook googling statewide movers. I was also booking a flight for me to go to Miami in two weeks to find me a house. I wasn't playing with this nigga any more, he could go play with some baby dolls. "BAE, come here," he shouted from the front. Kissing my teeth I got up to see what he wanted before his loud ass disturbed my babies. I walked to the front to see him with his hand around the back of his "girls" throat and her face looking like she saw a ghost.

"Come here she got some shit to say to you. This was just a misunderstanding."

"I'm so sorry for coming to your home. It will never happen again, I didn't realize Scar had a family," suddenly her face turned purple and she choked some. "I mean I have the wrong house and the wrong nigga. Someone was using his name, I haven't been fucking your man." Her eyes told a different story, one of fear and confusion. Her tears flowed long and deep like the river Nile. He dropped her to the concrete steps where she jumped up and ran off down the road.

Shaking my head I clapped my hands together and forced out a dry ass laugh. "Great show Scar, you get better with age. If that's all I have shit to do," I said turning around. He snatched my arm forcing me to look at him. I don't know for what because all I saw standing before me was a nigga who would never be shit. After all we had been through, a baby, the bitches, the fights this was the best he could do to try and make shit right.

"Come on Xa, what's the fucking problem now ma? I don't appreciate the attitude. Hell she told you what the fuck was up and now you still walking around here big mad. What you need from me now, a new car? Or another fucking bag to collect dust in the closet? Or maybe some more diamonds? Just let a nigga know so I can make it happen and we can move on."

He looked at me like I was an inconvenience to him, like I was mad just to be mad. I guess I made this shit up in my head. Or I was acting up for some materialistic shit. "You know what I want from you Scar, I want you to leave me the fuck alone. You think because you roughed up the girl you been fucking after she came to my house and told me I was your side chick that I'm supposed to what be grateful? Jump around for fucking joy? Nigga you got this shit so fucked up. I have told you time and time again I was getting tired but you can't think with anything else but your funky ass dick. You think being a bully and disrespecting other women is what I want from my children's father?" I had to take a few shallow breaths because suddenly my throat closed and I couldn't breathe at all. Forcing myself to calm down I sagged against the wall hoping it would hold me up.

"As for me wanting you to buy me jewels or cars or Gucci bags, nigga I don't want it. Save it. If I want a new whip I will find another nigga, one better than you to buy it for me." I watched his eyes turn totally black as he grabbed me by my throat and shoved me further into the wall that had become my crutch. I was looking into the eyes of the devil and he had lost control. He let me go but didn't move his body from in front of me.

"Xanaya Dream Carter you belong to me, don't you ever in your life talk to me about another nigga doing shit for you, near you or with you. I will kill both of ya'll."

"Mommy crying," Favour said standing next to us both with tears in his little confused eyes. Snatching my son in my arms I moved as fast as I could to get Sci and get the hell out of Scars path.

"I'm sorry Xa, I didn't mean to hurt you," Scar cried out behind me. But it was too late. He never meant to hurt me but somehow he always did. I spent the rest of the day in the living room with my kids online prepping for my move away from NY and way from Scar.

I sat up sipping Grey Goose and Patron after I got the kids to bed. I decided I should get some sleep soon but didn't know where to sleep. Scar had been dragging his pitiful ass around the house all day and he was in our room right now. Taking a shower in the kid's room I slid on some pink shorts and a white tank top I found in the laundry and headed to Kevon's room. I slid in to bed next to him and pulled him close. He wrapped his arms around me in his sleep and smiled. Gently I placed a kiss on his forehead and drifted off to sleep.

Scar

Seeing Xanaya sleeping on Kevon's little as twin bed made my heart break. She would rather sleep in here than be next to me. I did her dirty and I knew it. I picked her up and she snuggled into my body in her sleep. I hadn't even been home for the last three nights. I was too busy hanging out in the traps letting bitches suck me off and give me threesomes. That hood celebrity shit never got old to me. I always told Xa I was out on business but hell she was smart she knew I didn't really have to go to the traps to do shit but collect money and make sure everything was straight. I spent enough time in there these days I should have saved the team some money and not even paid no workers. I could have did that shit myself.

As soon as I laid Xanaya down on the bed her eyes popped open and she began to struggle against me trying to get up. "Baby come on just relax. Let me show you how sorry I am." I pleaded as I began kissing her neck and then the top of her breasts. As soon as I made my way to her navel her pretty ass eyes began to roll in the back of her head.

Slowly I pulled her shorts down and just sat back and admired her freshly waxed pussy. My girl pussy was always on point. Even after two kids her body was the shit, she had that snapback but I would have loved her even if she had kept some of the baby weight on her. I flicked my tongue over her clit as she began moaning out loud I went harder and faster.

I stuck two fingers in her tight ass hole and she began

bucking against my fingers urging me on. Nibbling on her treasure she grabbed my head and pushed me further into her. I could feel her tighten around my fingers and I knew she was about to squirt. I made sure I had my mouth all over he when she erupted and I licked up all her cum before I started all over again. I wanted to fuck, hell it felt like my dick was going to explode but I needed to make this moment all about her. It was the only way aside from buying her shit and busting a cap in niggas that I knew how to show her I loved her. Stopping I rubbed her nub and watched her face as she made her cum faces. Right when her mouth formed an O I knew she was cumming again. "Xnaya I love you," I said before I kissed her second set of lips catching all her nectar.

I crawled up her body and leaned on my side watching her. Even with her eyes closed in sleep I could see she was in emotional pain. Her face was swollen from all the crying and the red marks from where I choked her earlier were there. I wished I could take back every fucked up thing I had ever done to her but I couldn't. I also wished I truly could promise her I wouldn't fuck up again, but I couldn't. I knew I should let Xanaya go, let her find a man who would treat her right but I just couldn't.

*****

The night I thought about letting Xa go was the last night I was close to her. A week later and she was still sleeping in the kids rooms when I was there or the couch. On the real I knew I had to grow the fuck up and fast or I was going to lose my family. Looking out in the yard I leaned up against the door frame and watched as Xanaya chased Kevon and Favour while holding our one and a half year old daughter Sciniya in her arms. I never loved her more than I did at this moment. She was so beautiful to me her eyes were shining with happiness and joy. She was such a great mom. She was just happy spending time with our kids, not for any other reason. I always thought it would be me and her, I took that for granted. Shit I never thought I would want to settle down and I never really did, until now. And to be honest with myself it was probably to fucking late. I also never thought Xanaya would really leave me. Not like this, she wasn't thinking about getting her own place or moving across town. After last week shit had got real.

I saw the houses that Xa was looking at online and the schools for Kevon in Miami. I even snuck and read the texts between her and her girls about her packing up the kids and leaving me without a word. I felt like a straight pussy reading texts and shit. She told them she was she was done and I believed her. When Cassy showed up on my doorstep I was pissed the fuck off. All the times I had cheated and did bullshit no girl had ever come to our home and did no foul shit like that. Slowly I had noticed that Xanaya was going through all the kids' old clothes and taking them to the donation center. She was cleaning out the basement and closets. The time was coming and I wasn't letting go of my girl and kids without a fight.

Holding the door opened for her I helped the kids with their shoes and jackets. We had been living in this eerie silence for six and a half days now and I knew something had to give. At least we weren't arguing, but I felt like this shit was worse. Catching her at the fridge I crept up behind her. Seeing the look of fear on her face made me feel some sort of way. Xa had never looked at me with fear before even after I held a gun to her head. "Ma look I'm not trying to be on no fuck shit or argument type bullshit. We just need to talk. I know I hurt you and me saying sorry is old but we gotta communicate and work out something because we got these kids. I know you leaving me Xa, I saw the houses, the movers and shit. Just let's figure out something so I know what's up." She stood still for a few minutes and nodded her head.

"Ok, let's talk after the kids go down because I don't want them in the middle of the fussing we always doing. They deserve better than that even if I don't."

"Cool," I said in agreement. It hurt me that she felt I didn't think she deserved better than fighting with her nigga all the time. If that was the case I wouldn't be letting her go. I swear the day went slower than fuck after that. I went over some of my finances and shit to prepare for the moves I was going to have to make. Then I played with the boys until they passed out on the living room floor. I felt nervous to talk to Xanaya for the first time since I met her. She was in the living room with some white bootie shorts on and a colorful sports bra. Her yoga mat was on the ground and she was doing the downward dog. Shit I wanted to jump behind her and fuck her brains out but I knew that wasn't gonna fly, so I just watched her for a while.

She got up to turn off the DVD and saw me standing there. "Damn Scar you been there long? I forgot you wanted to talk you should have said something," she continued. After she drank some water and wiped her face with a mini towel she plopped down on the couch. "Shit you gonna talk or just watch me," she asked with an attitude. The one I missed so much. When she didn't beat the shit out of Cassy the day she popped up I knew Xanaya had reached her breaking point. It was easier for me to justify my actions when she was beating up bitches and fighting my ass. Her ratchet behavior made for a good excuse for my womanizing ways. It just seemed fair, like we were both on some constant bullshit.

"Xanaya look. I know I'm wrong for everything. I have no excuses, no explanation that could explain my fucked up behavior. I was a boy Xa, I acted like a boy and I'm ready to change." She was about to say some smart shit but I couldn't let this conversation go left. I had to keep her listening and not arguing. "Look please just give me a chance to speak please. Respect me because I respect you."

She rolled her eyes but nodded and I got on my knees in front of her so I was leaning into her and we were face to face. "Xa I love you, I don't know how to show it but I love yo ass. You mean everything to me and I realize how much I been hurting you. So Xa I love you enough to let you go. I know you want to go to Miami and I just ask that you let us move down there together. You can have your own spot and I will respect your privacy but I don't want to be away from my kids. I can't be away from them and honestly Xa I don't want to be away from you. I'm letting you go for now but someday when you see I'm a better man I'm getting you back." I leaned in and kissed her and to my surprise she kissed me back.

Sarai

The move to Miami was a good one. Shit New York had nothing but horror stories for me. I was sad when we had to leave Xanaya but then Scar was Scar and they ended up down here too. I transferred to University of Miami and only had one year left before I got my Bachelors in Social Work. Mulan was having the time of her life, especially now that she had her daddy with her daily. Oh and not to mention a great grandmother who loved her unconditionally. We sent papers to Fabian asking him to sign over his rights to Mulan so Lynk could adopt her and he sent them back the next day notarized. I guess he really had no interest in being a father or he was scared of Lynk either way it worked out. Mulan got Lynks last name and was issued a new birth certificate. Good thing Fabian made the smart choice because Lynk was ready to murder his ass if he had to.

    I sat back and thought about the dumb shit I used to do and I learned to no longer hate myself for any of that. I had no regrets because all I had been through made me the woman I was today. I can say I learned from my mistakes and I was going to make sure my kids didn't make the same ones. Hearing the door downstairs I knew it was the girls coming to pick me up. We were going to dinner and then to do some shopping for Christmas. I adjusted the bun I had put my Havana twists in and smoothed the teal and cream off the shoulder flowered dress. I added my tall cream leather boots and a jean jacket since it got chilly in the winter time down here. I swear I didn't miss snow one fucking bit.

Slowly I walked downstairs and smiled when I saw everyone was there. "Auntie pretty," Tamir said running up to me wanting to give me a hug. He was the sweetest baby ever I swear. Favour followed not wanting his big cousin to be doing something he wasn't.

Lynk walked up and cuffed both of them in the back of the head. "Ya'll little niggas get off my girl. She don't want loving from no one but me." Everybody laughed at the serious look on his face. Being with Lynk made me happy even though he still had a lot of insecurities about being in a relationship. I could see the fear when he would get mad or we would argue. I always reassured him that what happened in his past was not who he was now. "Shorty where you going in that little ass dress and boots, you shopping in that shit," he asked me his eyes looking all crazy. The old me would have been intimidated but the new me just reached up and kissed him.

"Babe you jealous," I laughed until he pulled me closer and I could feel his hard dick against me. "Don't be following us and shit," I said because he would do something like that. He has done shit like that.

"Girl don't make me kill nobody out here," he whispered in my ear. He reached in his jeans and handed me a knot of money. I took it and gave him one more kiss. Lynk made sure I didn't want for shit and I was finally comfortable letting him take care of me. Especially now, we were tied together for life.

"Damn ewww ya'll so damn nasty, we already running late wit yo slow ass so come one. That's how her ass got knocked up to begin with" Xanaya couldn't help but to talk shit. Mya just got up laughing as she kissed Tsunami and snatched more money from him. I knew he gave her ass some earlier. She was a spoiled brat.

"Xa come get some of this money," Scar said.

"Naw I'm good, I got my own money," she said rolling her eyes his way and kissing her kids. He still shoved it in her Louie bag before he stalked outside with a big ass attitude. I swear those two would never change. I wanted to see them make it but every day it seemed less and less likely. Since they been out here Xanaya turned into an Instagram celebrity and really didn't need him. She was making racks just to show up at parties and other events.

"Xa don't be so hard on him," I said because I knew deep down inside she still loved him. And I knew he loved the shit out of her. I could see the loneliness in her though. She barely dated or anything, seemed like no man she met was the right one because they weren't Scar.

She flipped me the bird but still walked back to the doorway and said something to him. She gave him an intimate hug that he ended by palming her ass, before she came to the truck. As we climbed into Mya's Rang Rover I rubbed my baby bump and closed my eyes. I wanted the best for my friends, shit they were more than that to me. They were the only family I had in this world. Really all any of us had was each other and I was thankful we all ended up settling close together. For the first time ever I was completely happy with my life and I knew the best was yet to come.

Lynk

I sat on the edge of the bed watching Sarai get ready. She fit the designer dress like a glove. Her small pregnant belly looked adorable and didn't interrupt the flow of the soft gold material. "Babe you sure you want me to come to this meeting with you," she asked? I could see the insecurity in her eyes. I had never took her to any of the business meetings I had to attend in the past. She knew I used to always bring Michelle but me not bringing her wasn't because I felt like Michelle was more than her. In my eyes Sarai was everything and I wanted to hide her away from the world and keep her safe. Introducing her to the other side of my life meant opening her up to the dangers of dating a drug lord. But since she was now my one and only I knew the time would have to come.

I walked over to her and kissed the nape of her neck. We looked so good together my black tux looked like new money and was only interrupted by the bling from my earrings and Rolex. With her heels on she came almost to my shoulder and she was matching my fly with her tear drop diamond earrings and matching necklace. "Babe come on now with the insecure bullshit. You wit me, you got me and I always want you by my side. We over here looking like the hood Obamas and shit, you bout to make me say fuck this dinner. We can just stay home and fuck because you got a nigga on brick."

"Well at least I aint rocking no more Forever Twenty One outfits," she said giving off an odd laugh. I still remembered the shit she was talking about and I knew deep down it bothered her.

"Ma listen to me, I wouldn't give a fuck if you had on the ninety nine cent special from Walmart. I would still rock wit you and still want to bend that ass over right here, right now. I fell in love wit you when you were rocking Forever Twenty One and Rainbow gear. You my shorty and that's for life."

She stopped for a minute and thought about what she was going to say. I loved that about Sarai. She never just said the first thing that came to mind like rude ad Xanaya. "You didn't sleep again last night," she said lowly.

Gripping her shoulders I pushed her against the dresser and got in her face. "It's not you. Stop over thinking shit." I wasn't going to say shit else but I knew I had to start giving her honesty. Running my hand over my goatee I sighed. "Look I still have a lot of issues. It just is what it is ma. Having a baby, being a father, that shit scares the fuck out of me. All the shit I been through, killing Misa and my unborn, killing my mother it haunts me. I aint going no fucking where I just have to work my way through this shit, just know I love yo ass and I love our kids. Now bring that sexy ass on and show ya man something on the ride."

She grabbed my dick and laughed, "I got you," she said smirking. I could see the relief in her eyes and I was glad I came at her straight instead of hiding the shit that I was struggling wit. Walking out to the limo I let the driver open the door and I helped Sarai in. She pulled out a little towel from her purse and went to unzipping my pants. As soon as I felt her warm mouth on my dick I moaned. She knew how to get me right. "You like that shit baby," she said before she deep throated my shit. I was straight fucking her mouth hoping this bitch ass driver wasn't listening. His ass I would murder with no regard.

She had spit running down my balls as she made

sure it got sloppy just how I liked it. I wasn't even paying attention to anything going on around me all I could think about was busting. Finally I couldn't take no more. Grabbing her shoulders I tried to lift her up but she kept going until all my seeds swam down her throat. I swear she was freaky as shit since she got pregnant. "Damn girl you know a nigga not ever heating on yo ass."

"Shit I know if you don't want me to kill yo behind," she said giving me a serious ass look as she rinsed her mouth out with some mini mouthwash shit she had. I just bit her neck and smirked. I knew that pussy was leaking but she had to wait until later.

We arrived at the beach side mansion belonging to the head of the Columbian connect that my uncle used to partner with. I couldn't bring myself to think of that nigga as my pops even though I knew he would. "Lynk, it has been a very long time my friend," Cabos greeted me as I entered the double doors.

"It has, I see life has been good to you," I responded with a smile. Cabos had always been a good dude. He wasn't greedy like so many in this business. I could see his eyes wander over Sarai from head to toe.

"I see you have a new girl, she is lovely if you don't mind me saying." I could see the lust in his eyes. See this why I wanted to keep Sarai ass out the spotlight. Cabos wouldn't be the last. I knew I did good bringing two guns instead of one.

"Fuck yea I mind you saying. Don't be fucking looking at her or thinking shit," I said. I knew my eyes were looking crazy as fuck I couldn't hold my temper when it came to Sarai for shit. Pulling her closer I let one of my hands go towards my waste. She put her hand on my arm trying to tell me to chill.

"No disrespect Lynk, I can see this one is special. Congrats on the baby by the way," he said as he stuck out his hand for me to shake. I guess no one had ever seen me be serious about a female before so they didn't expect this. Shaking his hand I led Sarai to a table in the back hoping no one would make me end their life tonight. The dinner seemed to drag on and on. I shook more wrinkled old hands tonight than ever in life. Now that my pops was dead this was all on me. All the fake smiles and ass kissing from one man to another only for everyone to go back to their territory and try to outdo the other person. I was over it, but I was stuck. This was my life, and even if I wanted to my soul was committed and I couldn't walk away. I watched the way Sarai spoke with the women in attendance and I knew I had made a good choice bringing her. She was classy and sweet, she didn't have to pretend to be anyone else her real personality made everyone fall in love with her.

Checking the time I knew we had to leave soon. I had somewhere else for us to be and I didn't want to be late. Interrupting her conversation with a few ladies who hung on her every word I kissed her on the cheek. "Babe it's time to go so wrap this up," I said. I stood there while she said her goodbyes.

"I hope we going home to fuck since you want to be rushing me out of here and shit." She side eyed me with a hopeful look in her eyes.

I slapped her ass, "dam girl you horny as fuck. What you going to do when I have to leave town?" Her look turned into a glare and she crossed her arms in a pout once she settled in the back of the limo. We drove for a while until we made it to Vizcaya Gardens. I had never been here before but Mama picked it out when I told her what I wanted to do and looking at how nice the view was I knew she had did the right thing. It cost a fortune to rent this place for an evening but the look on Sarai's face would be worth every penny. Just proves money really does talk.

"Where are we babe, we bought to fuck here? I don't mind some public sex." Sarai was a mess these days. Gone was the shy beat down girl that I met in church. She caused me to grin so hard I know she was looking all in my platinum grill. Mushing me in the face she went back to poking out her lips and shit. "You make me sick, you all happy and shit because you got yours and I'm walking around here with a wet ass pussy no relief in sight." She rolled those pretty brown eyes and for real turned her head on a nigga to look out the window with an attitude. "And I aint getting out this fucking car either," she threw over her shoulder.

"Come on ma, damn you need zaddy dick that bad and shit," I asked her joking? She nodded her head and looked like she wanted to cry. Texting the driver to park and take a walk I knew I had to make it right for my baby. Unzipping my pants I grabbed her and hiked up her gown. Licking the top of her breasts I popped one out of her dress and bit her nipple. "You so fucking sexy Rai, come get this dick ma." As soon as I felt her bomb as pregnant pussy I swear nothing could have stopped me from fucking the shit out of her. She started riding my shit like a porn star.

"Yes Lucifer I love this dick. I'm about to cum all over your shit." She was yelling and digging her nails in my neck. I grabbed her round ass and made sure she felt all of me. That shit must have hit her spot because she came so hard tears fell out her eyes and made her make up run. I didn't waste no more time as I bust a big ass nut. If she wasn't already pregnant that would have been some fucking twins. Every time I was in her pussy I regretted fighting this shit between us for so long. She collapsed against me and kissed my neck. "I love you," she whispered and a nigga felt his heart beating extra fast and shit.

"I love you too ma," I hated to ruin the moment but we had to get ourselves together. Wiping up as best I could we fixed our clothes and walked down the path to some stone bridge, it led to a little mosque looking room at the end. I held her hand so she didn't fall with the heels she had on. Once we got inside it was dead ass quiet even though the room was full, all our friends where there and all the kids. Even Scars Grams and cousins stood watching us. Mulan ran from Mama and jumped in my arms. "Hey my favorite girl," I said as I kissed her. Handing her to Xanaya I low key grabbed the ring box from her at the same time. Sarai looked around in confusion and I knew I had to move fast before she said something. For the first time ever I was nervous. I felt my palms get sweaty.

Turning towards Sarai I watched the sun set behind us and I knew the time was right. The pastor stood in the shadows where she couldn't see him. Dropping to my knee I pulled out the little velvet box and opened the top. "Sarai you came into my life and changed me. I never thought a woman would truly love me or that I could love her but you were that woman. There was never a time I didn't want you by my side I was just scared. I did everything wrong while thinking I was doing everything right. You have given me more than I deserve and I will never stop loving you, never leave your side. I will be there through whatever and kill any nigga for you. Sarai Marie Andrews will you marry me?" She nodded yes as I slid the ring on her finger, and for the second time as a grown man I cried.

Kahmya

Standing up I smoothed my hand over the light gauzy fabric that covered my torso and flowed out around my knees. The dress was accented in soft pink rhinestones that matched the soft pink color painted on my toes and nails. Not a traditional outfit for what I was about to do but nothing about this day would be traditional. Slowly making my way downstairs I took a deep breath. Today was about me and Tsunami, no one else. Looking out the sliding glass door I watched him standing there bathed in the moonlight. I was speechless looking at him. He only had on white linen pants rolled up so the bottoms wouldn't get wet. His dreads were twisted up into a ponytail on top of his head. He held Kasai against his bare chest her ruffled white dress was probably itching his skin but I couldn't tell by his relaxed stance. Tamir played in the sand next to him most likely ruining his own white pants, but I was learning that was what little boys did. Those three, they were all I needed which was why I couldn't find the words to describe how I felt. I guess if I had to pick one emotion it would be at peace, finally I was at peace in my life.

In the distance I could see the pastor's silhouette as he held the Bible patiently waiting as I walked out to meet my destiny. I had prayed for this for so long, even before I knew what I was praying for. All those talks with God about unconditional love, security and happiness did not go in vain. My day had come.

"You ready," Tsunami asked as he turned to me? I could see nothing but love in his eyes. The same love that had always been there, when I was broken he loved me just the same and that meant everything to me. Slipping my hand into his I felt my bare feet sink further into the silky sand as we made our way to the beachside. I never pictured this day but I wouldn't change it. So what that Tsunami was walking me down the white fabric we had used as an aisle instead of some unknown father. So what that it was just us, I wanted it that way.

There was a full moon tonight, it seemed like it was shining just for me. Like an approval from God himself. As we stopped in front of the Pastor I lifted my head to the sky and whispered "thank you lord".

Pastor Jenks began the ceremony. I was glad he skipped the *we are gathered here today* spiel since it was just us. "Jesus Christ Reminds us that at the beginning the Creator made us male and female, and said, for this cause a man shall leave his father and mother and shall cleave to his wife; and the two shall become one flesh.

God loved us, and created us to love others. Our lives find completion only as we love and are loved in return. Together, we can become what we could never be separately. Marriage is of God.

God wants us to know that love is patient, love is kind. It does not envy, it does not boast, it is not proud. It is not rude, it is not self-seeking, it is not easily angered, it keeps no record of wrongs. Love does not delight in evil but rejoices with the truth. It always protects, always trusts, always hopes, and always perseveres. Love never fails.

Kahmya and Tsunami come today desiring to be united in this sacred relationship.

"Let us Pray," he said and I felt a chill go through my body as I bowed my head.

"Almighty God you have created us all in the image of Love, the image of yourself. Bless now these two who stand before you. Guide them in your wisdom, shine your light upon them, that as they journey through this life together they will walk as bearers of your Truth. Amen."

"Amen," me and Tsu said at the same time. That caused me to smile up at him.

Pastor Jenks asked us to, "Please join hands," and I felt my hand slide effortlessly into his once again. I thought of all the times he held my hand over the years. When I was six and was too afraid to cross the street and go to the store by myself. The first time I snuck out of the bed with Creek and sat in the dark hallway and cried all night. Then when I was in labor, scared an in pain with both of our kids, he was there still holding my hand. It was symbolic. "I know you bot have your own vows if you would like to proceed."

I took a deep breath because I was going first. I had wrote this long two page run down of all the ways I loved Tsunami and wanted to spend my life with him but I decided to just speak from the heart. Looking into his brown eyes I began to get lost. "Tsunami, declarations of love cannot be rehearsed or thought of in pretense. The love I have for you cannot even be put into words. My heart beats for you Tsunami, aside from the appreciation I have for you it's so much more. I have given you things I have never given any other man. You have my trust, my loyalty, my mind, body and soul. I will spend every day for the rest of my life showing you how much I love you." We were both crying when I finished. I guess my words even affected Tamir because he was holding still and gazing at us a smile on his small face.

Tsunami

As a man I felt like today, this moment was a defining moment in my life. This was what I wanted, to spend my life with Mya, there was no question in my mind or heart. I was still the same nigga, the one who would hustle, kill or go to the end of the world to protect her. Pastor Jenks and Mya were staring at me, waiting for me to say my vows. I cleared my throat a few times and it sounded strange in the silence of the night. I was never one for all the romantic shit but I wanted Mya to know how I really felt. She squeezed my hand trying to offer me strength. It was cute coming from her. I squeezed back and thought about how far we had come. I never thought life would have taken us through so much and that we would have ended up here together.

"Kahmya, I want you to know that pain is what allows us to love. All the pain you have been through, all the pain I have felt for you is what makes our love real. I have never doubted for a moment that I loved you, not when you made me mad or frustrated. I always knew I would do anything for you and I always will. I promise to always give you the best of me, to fight any battle with you and to never leave your side. You will always get the best of me Mya, for the rest of my life."

I vaguely heard the Pastor pronounce us man and wife as I slid her ring on her finger and leaned in for my kiss. This kiss felt like so much more, her lips met mine, soft and fluffy. I slid my tongue in her mouth and began exploring. I didn't want to stop but Pastor Jenks cleared his throat. Looking up he looked a little embarrassed at all the public affection. Shrugging I pulled Mya close so her breasts brushed my bare chest. I couldn't wait until I could get her back to the hotel and dig all in her guts. She was getting pregnant again tonight. I winked at her as we all said one final prayer.

"Thank you Pastor, the ceremony was perfect," I said as he left us on the beach. Mya took the baby from me and I picked up Tamir. He laid his head on my shoulder and popped his thumb in his mouth. I could feel his breathing getting heavy and I knew he would be sleeping soon. Slowly we walked towards the water until we could feel the waves flowing over our feet. "Thank you Kahmya," I said looking out into the ink black water interrupted only by the light from the move.

"For what Tsu," she asked stepping closer to my side so our kids were snuggled in between us?

"For letting me be the one to love you."

Xanaya

Walking in the house I kicked off my heels at the door and let out a moan of relief. I was happy that the time I needed to be at the new club Zero wasn't as late as I usually had to stay. My feet hurt like fuck and I was just plain tired. Taking care of three kids on my own was starting to wear me down. I knew I could have hired a nanny, or asked they daddy or the girls for more help but I was on my independent shit. I hadn't fucked Scar for months, hell since before we had moved here and even though it was hard I was proud of myself for breaking whatever crazy, toxic cycle we had.

I would be lying though if I didn't admit I missed him. I didn't just miss him dicking me down but I missed having my friend, my partner around. Sitting back on the couch I thought back to all the good times we had. I spent so much time with him in the trap or on the block. Those days we were inseparable. We stayed cracking jokes on the people out in the hood or even on each other. Some days I didn't know if I could ever move on fully. I still slept in his t-shirts at night. I would sneak over to Grams house when he wasn't home and steal shirts out of his hamper so they smelled like his cologne.

Smiling at the comfort the shirts brought me I made my way upstairs to shower. It was quiet so I figured everyone was asleep, Grams had stayed and watched the kids for me. After a hot shower I pulled on the white tee I had snatched two days ago and a pair of silk peach panties. Collapsing on my bed I closed my eyes. "God, I miss him so much. I see him improving every day and I swear I am happy he is. But it breaks my heart to know he wouldn't improve for me. I wonder what girl got him out here acting right. And God I know it's terrible but I hate her. What is wrong with me that he just couldn't love me?"

If I was honest with myself I was so tired because of this. I couldn't sleep at night. I was broken, I just hid it well. I felt the tears, so hot they burned my eyes as I pleaded with God for understanding and comfort. Feeling the bed creek I almost jumped out of my fucking skin as my eyes flew open. There he was in the flesh, the man I still loved.

"What the hell Scar you damn near gave me a heart attack," I sassed trying to wipe my tears away but they just wouldn't stop coming.

"Sorry, I was here hanging out with the kids so I sent Gram home earlier. She wanted to hit up Bingo in the morning. I didn't mean to scare you."

Slowly I nodded my head. Grams loved Bingo especially in Florida. She said she always won here. I gazed at Scar out of my blurry eyes. He looked better than ever, he had let his hair grow out some and it was now in tight little curls all over his head. He had on some white Versace shorts and a black and white shirt to match. I could smell his Armani cologne from where I was and it had my pussy throbbing.

"Come here," he said as he pulled me closer to him in his strong arms. He made me straddle him and I dropped my head to his chest soaking his chest. "Stop fucking crying Xa, you aint got to do that shit. I told you a long time ago I always got you. I heard what you said and it's like you don't understand how I feel about yo ass. I love you," he grabbed my chin and forced my head up. I tried to drop it back so he couldn't see how I felt. "Naw look at me Xanaya. I love you! If you see me changing, trying harder, growing the fuck up it's because of you. I aint move out here chasing no bitch but you, I never want you to think anything I'm doing is about anyone else. It never will be. Just give me another chance Xa. Please a nigga begging you."

I didn't know what to say, I felt like my heart was in my throat and I couldn't speak at all. Climbing out of his arms I started to take my panties off so he could fuck the shit out of me. Feeling his strong hand on mine he stopped me. "Naw, it aint about that. Come on, let me just hold you, we can fuck and do all that shit later on. I'm trying to show you how much I care."

I crawled up to the top of my king size bed as he took off his clothes. Sliding under the covers he followed and pulled me against his chest. "I love you Scar," I whispered.

"I love you more Xa."

The End!!!

Made in United States
North Haven, CT
12 January 2025